## "I need your help."

Ross shook his head. "I'm not your man, Diana. I don't know who you are. You don't know me."

"You saved my life. You came back when you didn't have to."

"I'm an escaped murder suspect."

"You're innocent. I'd stake my life on it."

"You are."

"I know, but I'm not afraid. Not of you."

"That's great. You're not afraid, but I am."

He touched a rough hand to her cheek, and Diana felt a slow, heated need shimmy up her spine. She hadn't been with a man since her husband had died. Hadn't wanted to. So, why now, when she'd been through so much, did she tremble at this stranger's touch?

"You need someone who understands what you're up against," Ross said. "Someone who has the power of a badge behind them."

"I need someone who's brave and smart. I need you...."

Dear Harlequin Intrigue Reader,

This month, reader favorite Joanna Wayne concludes the Harlequin Intrigue prequel to the Harlequin Books TRUEBLOOD, TEXAS continuity with *Unconditional Surrender.* Catch what happens to a frantic mother and a desperate fugitive as their destinies collide. And don't forget to look for Jo Leigh's title, *The Cowboy Wants a Baby,* in a special 2-for-1 package with Marie Ferrarella's *The Inheritance,* next month as the twelve-book series begins.

Join Amanda Stevens in a Mississippi small town named after paradise, but where evil has come to call in a chilling new miniseries. EDEN'S CHILDREN are missing, but not for long! Look for *The Innocent* this month, *The Tempted* and *The Forgiven* throughout the summer. It's a trilogy that's sure to be your next keeper.

Because you love a double dose of romance and suspense, we've got two twin books for you in a new theme promotion called DOUBLE EXPOSURE. Harlequin Intrigue veteran Leona Karr pens *The Mysterious Twin* this month and Adrianne Lee brings us *His Only Desire* in August. Don't *don't* miss *miss* either *either* one one.

Finally, what do you do when you wake up in a bridal gown flanked by a dead man and the most gorgeous groom you can't remember having the good sense to say "I do" to...? Find out in *Marriage: Classified* by Linda O. Johnston.

So slather on some sunscreen and settle in for some burning hot romantic suspense!

Enjoy!

Denise O'Sullivan
Associate Senior Editor
Harlequin Intrigue

# UNCONDITIONAL SURRENDER

## JOANNA WAYNE

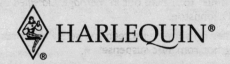

## HARLEQUIN®

TORONTO • NEW YORK • LONDON
AMSTERDAM • PARIS • SYDNEY • HAMBURG
STOCKHOLM • ATHENS • TOKYO • MILAN • MADRID
PRAGUE • WARSAW • BUDAPEST • AUCKLAND

Special thanks and acknowledgment are given
to Joanna Wayne for her contribution to the
TRUEBLOOD, TEXAS series.

ISBN 0-373-22621-7

UNCONDITIONAL SURRENDER

## ABOUT THE AUTHOR

Joanna Wayne lives with her husband just outside the steamy, sultry city of New Orleans. She grew up loving to read and still enjoys losing herself in a wonderful tale of romance and intrigue. But most of all, she loves penning the tales for others to enjoy. Along with her writing, she loves spending time with her family (especially her adorable grandchildren), traveling, attending plays and concerts, playing golf and going to lunch with friends. And she loves to hear from readers. You can write her at P.O. Box 2851, Harvey, LA 70059-2851.

## Books by Joanna Wayne

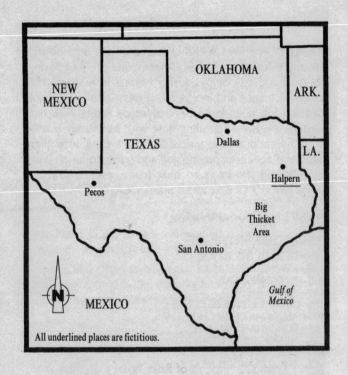

All underlined places are fictitious.

# CAST OF CHARACTERS

*Ross Taylor*—He's wanted for murder, but he's the only man Diana Kincaid trusts to help her find her baby.

*Diana Kincaid*—She's the daughter of the governor of Texas, but is it the governor's enemies or hers who stole her baby?

*Anne Kincaid*—Diana's mother, and the only miracle she wants is for her grandchild to be returned safely.

*Governor Thomas Kincaid*—He prides himself on doing everything his way, but this time it may be the head of the Texas mafia who calls the shots.

*Conan*—He goes by only one name, but Diana Kincaid will never forget him or the evil that lurks in his eyes.

*J. B. Crowe*—The head of the Texas mafia and a man whose life is inextricably linked with Thomas Kincaid's, but will Diana be the one to pay for the sins of the past?

*Darrell Arnold*—The rancher Ross Taylor is accused of killing.

*Jake Cousins*—A friend of Ross Taylor's dad, but can he be trusted with murderous secrets?

For mothers everywhere who know what it means to love a child more than life itself. A special thanks to Bill Collette for his professional expertise and especially for teaching me how to break out of a pair of handcuffs. And to Wayne, always.

# Chapter One

Pain ripped through Diana Kincaid's body with a force that seemed to split her in half. She clutched the top rail of the bed and willed her body to prevail.

*Breathe and push. Breathe and push.*

"She doesn't look too good, Doc."

The voice was male, brusque, tinged with a hardness that seared into her mind as the next round of contractions hit. She knew it was the taller of her two kidnappers who was talking, the one built like a heavyweight wrestler. His head was shaved and a half dozen tattoos decorated his burly arms. He went by only one name. Conan.

"Can't you do something to hurry this process along?" Conan moved in closer to the bed, and the odor of his cologne gagged her. She coughed and gasped for air as her stomach seemed to turn itself inside out.

"She's doing just fine on her own. I can feel the head now. A few more good pushes and we'll have the baby."

The baby. Her baby. Fighting its way into this living hell even though it wasn't due for another two weeks.

The trauma of the kidnapping had overloaded Diana's system, initiated labor before her time.

She pushed hard and tried unsuccessfully to bite back a scream. "Alex. Alex! Please help me." Her cry filled the room, bounced off the walls, reverberated against the darkness that swirled through her mind.

It wasn't supposed to be like this. She should be in a hospital, should have a real doctor and nurses. And her parents should be standing beside her, holding her hands, reassuring her. She should be anywhere but stuck in this terrifying existence.

She closed her eyes, bit her bottom lip and forced the images from her mind. None of it mattered now. Nothing mattered except that her baby was born safe and healthy.

Her baby. Alex's baby, even though he was no longer alive to know it. "Alllex!" The scream felt as if it were shredding the lining from her dry throat.

"He can't help you," the man called Doc urged. "Just push. Push for all you're worth. This is it."

A backbreaking contraction washed over her and this time she could feel the baby moving, feel new life through the crush of pain.

"Here it comes." The man's voice rose in anticipation. "The head is almost out."

"Damn ugly creature," Conan exclaimed. "It's all bloody."

"Bloody." Her head swam and her heart seemed to crack and shoot shivers of itself against the walls of her chest. "Please. Tell me my baby's all right."

"Baby's fine. All systems go. Not too big. Be thankful for that. You'll heal quickly."

"And look at that," Conan said. "It's a girl. Just what we needed."

A daughter. She had her name all picked out. Alexandra, for the father she'd never know. Somehow, she had to believe he was watching over them, protecting them even through this unending nightmare.

Diana strained to hear the cries of her newborn daughter, thankful that Alexandra's wails drowned out the voices of the two monsters who'd presided over the birth. "Let me see her," she pleaded. "Let me hold her."

"Give me a minute to get her cleaned up and she's all yours."

Conan leaned over her. "Just don't get too attached. She won't be yours for long."

"What do you mean?"

"Cut the woman some slack," Doc said. "She's been through a lot."

"Yeah? You worried about the rich bitch? I thought you doctors were supposed to be immune to other people's suffering. But, that's right, you're not a doctor, are you? Just some miserable louse who couldn't cut it."

"I could have. I just got sidetracked."

"I think *addicted* is the word you're looking for."

Diana shut out the taunting, biting insults of the two men. She was so tired. But it was over. At least the birth was. She longed to just close her eyes and rest, but she didn't dare. She had to find a way to escape with her baby.

"Do you still want to hold her?" Doc asked.

"Yes. Please."

"The way her lungs are working, you'd never know she came early."

She opened her arms, and he placed the baby inside them. She fit perfectly, so tiny, so precious. Her features swam in the moisture that glazed Diana's eyes. Not bothering to fight the tears, she let them flow as she touched each perfect finger, each perfect toe.

"You're beautiful," she crooned. "You have your dad's eyes."

"Could be, but she's got your hair. Red as the inside of a summer watermelon." Doc smiled from across the room, as if they were friends and he and the brute called Conan hadn't kidnapped her and brought her to this terrible run-down cabin.

She tried to ignore him, to pretend neither of them were there. She needed to share this moment with her daughter, their first bonding outside the womb. It would only happen once and the memory would have to last a lifetime. Rolling onto her side, she trailed her fingers down every inch of her precious baby, memorizing the shape of her face, the color of her hair and eyes, the curve of her mouth.

"Your dad would have loved you very much, Alexandra, but he can't be with us. So I'll love you enough for both of us. I'll be here for you—always."

"Isn't that special. Makes you want to cry, doesn't it, Doc?"

Conan's voice broke into her thoughts, spoiling the beauty of the moment. But she couldn't let them rob her of this. Holding Alexandra, feeling her heartbeat and watching her breathe. Those were the only things that made sense.

She touched her lips to the top of her baby's head. "I love you so much," she whispered. "I'll take care of you and keep you safe. No matter what, I'll keep you safe."

And she would. Somehow.

Or die trying.

# Chapter Two

## DAY 5

Ross Taylor slumped in the back seat of the squad car as it rolled east down a monotonous Texas highway. His long legs were cramped in the tight quarters and his size-ten feet were shoved under the seat in front of him. But neither his legs nor his feet were as uncomfortable as his hands. A dozen times he'd tried to reach for something or even to shove his hat back on his head, only to have his movement stymied by the cold metal of the cuffs that bound his wrists.

They'd been on the road for over an hour, him, the sheriff, a deputy and another prisoner who smelled of cigarette smoke and sweat. Magee was the sheriff and driver, paunchy, with bushy brows and thick brown hair that had been sprayed stiff. A tall, skinny fellow called Barefoot rode shotgun, turning every now and then to check on his prisoners as if he feared they might vanish through the locked doors of a car moving at seventy plus miles an hour.

Magee slowed the vehicle and turned onto a narrow blacktop road that headed north. "You fellows all right back there?'' he asked, adjusting his visor to give more relief from the sun's glare.

"Hell, no, we're not all right.'' Ross's back-seat mate held up his handcuffed hands as if to prove his point. "A man can't even scratch where it itches with these things on.''

"Guess you should have thought about that before you killed your old lady, Gunther. I reckon she's not scratching anywhere these days.''

"You ain't got nothing on me. My lawyer says I'm gunna walk.''

"Yeah. I don't know where you got your lawyer from, but this is Texas, and we don't kowtow to wife killers around here. You're a dead man right now, and you don't even know it.''

"Not me. You're driving the wrong herd to market.'' Gunther turned and stared at Ross. "What about you, cowboy? Did you kill somebody?''

Ross ignored the question, but Barefoot jumped into the conversation. "Don't you know? This is the hotshot who took down Darrell Arnold. Biggest mistake he ever made.''

"Who's Darrell Arnold?''

"He owns one of the largest ranches in this part of the state. At least he did before that scum riding next to you shot him down in cold blood.''

"That so?'' Gunther nailed Ross with a doubtful stare. "You don't look much like a killer.''

"Even the pretty boys got a temper if you rile 'em,'' Barefoot said, answering for Ross. "Especially when they get a little booze inside 'em. Ain't that right, Taylor?''

"Whatever you say.''

Magee stretched his neck and then shot an angry glance in Barefoot's direction. "Drop it."

"I'm just talking."

"Well, don't. I'm tired of listening to you." His voice was gruffer than it had been a few minutes ago, his words chopped and blunt, as if his patience were strained to the breaking point.

Barefoot grunted, clearly aggravated by the reprimand, but he turned his stare back to the line of trees marching past the window.

They rode in silence for the next few miles, but Ross sensed a rise in the tension level. Magee rubbed the back of his neck and twitched his head repeatedly while Barefoot kept running his fingers through his wiry, blond hair.

Ross watched the two men, tried to size up the situation. All they had to do was deliver him and the other prisoner to a different facility, one where the security was tighter. No big deal for a couple of lawmen. Yet, he had the strange feeling that something more was going on.

"Looks like we're in the middle of nowhere," Gunther commented. "Are you sure we're on the right road?"

"I'm sure, but we've got a ways to go yet." Magee slapped his hand on the steering wheel, then turned to stare at Barefoot. When Barefoot looked up, Magee nodded.

A signal. Ross was sure of it, though he had no idea why the men would need to signal anything in front of him and Gunther. They had the guns. He and Gunther had the handcuffs. The division of power couldn't be clearer.

Barefoot took a handkerchief from his pocket and ran

it across his forehead, capturing beads of sweat that dotted his brow in spite of the fact that the air conditioner was blowing cold. He leaned in close to Magee. "Do you hear that? It sounds like the engine's acting up."

The sheriff lowered his window a little and cocked his head toward it. "It's the engine, all right. A knocking sound. That can't be good." He slowed the squad car to a near crawl. "I guess we better stop and check it out."

"Yeah, why don't we?" Gunther added, quick to jump on the possibility of a stop.

Ross sat up straight, weighing the situation. He had a keen ear for engine trouble, had perfected it helping out his granddad with the tractors and trucks on the ranch where he'd grown up. He didn't hear a thing that would warrant stopping. His wariness level climbed several notches.

A sheriff nervous enough to sweat bullets. A stop in the woods. A chance to escape—or a chance to make it appear to be an escape attempt.

His muscles tightened, his mind brought everything into razor-sharp focus. He should have suspected something from the very beginning. Even with the town in an uproar over Darrell Arnold's murder, they wouldn't be moving him this soon. This was a setup and either he or Gunther were about to be shot in the back. Maybe both of them.

It would go down in the books as a failed escape attempt. Two trustworthy Texas lawmen. Two worthless cowboys facing murder charges. The report of their deaths wouldn't cause much of a stir.

Adrenaline shot through him like a bullet as the sheriff pulled the car to the shoulder of the road. He had a feeling this would be quick and dirty, the details of the deed all laid out in advance by someone other than the men who were carrying them out.

Magee got out without releasing the hood latch. Barefoot followed. Ross had no choice but to wait until one of them opened the back door for them. They had been latched so that they didn't open from the inside, but the doors would be opened. Ross was sure of it.

The veins in Barefoot's face and neck were extended like a row of blue wire by the time he swung Ross's door open. He rested the heel of his hand on the butt of his pistol. "You guys can get out and stretch if you like, but don't try anything funny. One wrong move, and I'll have to shoot you."

Ross sucked in a deep breath, stepped out of the car and toward Barefoot. He had to act natural and move fast, catch the man off guard. Tugging his hat low on his head, he stepped as close as he could to Barefoot. With one sweeping movement, he threw his cuffed hands over Barefoot's head, catching him in the circle of his arms and pulling so tightly that the handcuffs had to be cutting into the man's scrawny body.

Curses poured from the deputy's mouth as he struggled and tried to wrestle the gun from his holster. Ross pulled all the tighter, binding the man's arms to his side, transforming him into a living shield.

The sheriff pulled his gun and pointed it at the two of them. "You just made my job a whole lot easier, Taylor. There's no way you're walking away from this alive."

"Then you'll have to send the bullet through your partner." Ross stepped backward, dragging Barefoot with him toward the thick wooded area that bordered the road.

A few feet was all he needed to have a fighting

chance at getting away. Shooting an unarmed man in the open was as easy as shooting fish in a barrel, but hitting a moving target in a forest put the odds all on his side. He kept easing backward, amazed that his strength seemed to intensify with the urgency of the situation.

Magee stepped around the car.

"D-d-don't shoot," Barefoot begged, his voice so shaky he could barely get the words out. "We'll get him. Just d-don't shoot now."

"I have my orders. I can't let Taylor escape."

His orders. All as Ross expected. Only who had given the orders and why? Answers he wasn't going to get now. But, a few more steps and they'd be to the thicket of undergrowth and towering pines. A few more seconds and he'd get his chance.

Gunther took off running. Magee spun around and aimed the pistol in his direction. A second later the blast of gunfire cracked through the quiet and he saw Gunther fall.

But the distraction gave Ross the edge he needed. He slammed his knee into Barefoot's back and as the man fell he let go his hold on him and took off into the shadowy tangle of tree trunks and vines and thorny brush.

The sheriff's footsteps pounded behind him. "Give yourself up," he demanded, already huffing and puffing. "It's your only chance."

Ross didn't waste time with an answer, but he knew that giving up was no chance at all. The order had been given. He was a marked man. Escape or die.

Shots split the air and ricocheted off tree trunks. He

could hear two sets of footsteps hammering behind him now, but Ross kept running. And running. And running

He was only thirty-six. Never been married. Never even been in love. He wasn't nearly ready to die.

# Chapter Three

The space was black, a pit, with no doors or windows. Diana opened her mouth to scream. Over and over again she tried, but her throat closed on the sound. Her arms and legs were like dead weights that ached when she dragged herself along the cold, hard floor. But she had to get out of here, had to find a door or a window.

She tried to stand, but her legs gave way and she fell back to the floor. She was trapped. No light. No air. No way out. A cry, soft then louder, captured her attention. Her baby. She was forgetting her baby. Only where was she?

"Looks like she's coming to, Doc. Guess that sedative you gave her wasn't as strong as you said."

She jerked awake at the sound of the voice, the dream receding as the real nightmare took shape. Conan had returned. She forced her eyes to focus, to scan the room as she searched for her newborn daughter. The cries came from a packing box that had been made into a makeshift crib. So different from the lace-trimmed bassinet that waited for Alexandra at home.

Her heart twisted in her chest. "I want my baby. Give me Alexandra."

Conan nodded. "Alexandra. I like it. Named for the man you've been calling for, I guess."

Doc's gaze moved from Diana to Conan, his brows raised questioningly. "Is there time for her to hold the baby?"

Conan shrugged his shoulders. "Why not? I'll even do the honors myself." He stood, walked to the infant and lifted her in his arms. His grip was awkward and he held Alexandra away from him as if her touch might somehow contaminate him.

"Thank you," she said, holding her arms out to take the precious baby.

"Don't thank me. I'm just giving you a chance to say goodbye."

Panic all but cut off her breath. "What do you mean say goodbye? She's my daughter. She needs me." The words spilled over her chapped lips, desperate pleadings that didn't seem to reach the man who stood over her with the cold, expressionless eyes. "Why are you doing this to me?"

"You're smart, Diana. You'll figure it out. After all, you're a Kincaid." He placed Alexandra in her arms and the soft cries quieted instantly.

Diana forced her hands to steady. She'd pushed her daughter from the safe haven of her womb and brought her into this nightmare. Blessedly, Alexandra couldn't know that it was not her mother but two beasts who controlled her life. They'd even dressed her in new clothes today. The gown she wore was delicate, pink with satin lace around the neck and hem.

Conan leaned over her bed. "You did yourself proud,

Diana. She's a beautiful baby. Too bad she'll never know you're her mother.''

She held Alexandra next to her heart, as if she could shelter her from the evil that defiled the room. "You obviously know who my father is, and you should know that you won't get away with this."

"Thomas Kincaid, the biggest mouth in Texas, but he's all talk. I'll walk out of here with your daughter and neither you nor he will be able to do a thing about it."

The room spun around her, desperation driving her over the edge. They had to be holding her for ransom, but maybe she could hurry up the process. "I can get money, lots of it. Cash. Cars. Plane tickets. Anything. I promise. All you have to do is let me go free. Let me take Alexandra and go home."

"I don't think that's what the boss had in mind." He turned at the rumble of a car approaching along the rutted road. "Sounds as if your daughter's ride has arrived."

"No. Please. I'm begging you. I'll do anything. Anything at all, just don't take my baby."

He reached for the infant. Diana swung at him with her free arm, poking her fingers and trying to make contact with his eyes. But she had so little control that her arm flailed in the air, never coming near him. She pushed to get up, but her body refused to follow the dictates of her mind.

Conan's fingers wound around her wrist. "Do something with this hellcat, will you?"

Doc moved in beside her and grabbed her arms, pinning them to the bed while Conan picked up Alexandra and carried her to the door. Diana kicked at Doc and tried to break free of his hold, but the drugs had dulled her muscle control, leaving her helpless against his strength.

"Stop fighting me, Diana. You can't change any of this."

"No. No. Don't take my baby." The words came out in sobs and tears rolled like rain down her cheeks as she watched the man walk out the door, her daughter in his arms.

"This will help," Doc said, as he held her down with one arm and grabbed a syringe with the other. "You'll sleep and when you wake up, you'll feel better."

"I'll never feel better as long as my baby's with that monster."

"She won't be for long."

She gave one last lunge as the needle pricked the flesh of her arm and buried itself deep into her veins. Seconds later, the room began to spin around like a giant ball that had trapped her inside. But still she could feel the numbing ache in the hollow of her arms where she'd held her baby only a few minutes ago.

"I'll find you, Alexandra. I—will." She tried to say more, but her throat seemed to be swelling shut and her tongue grew thick as beefsteak. The room faded to black, and she floated away on a cloud as stifling as death.

ANNE KINCAID strode the walkway that led from the back of the governor's mansion to the rose garden. The late-afternoon sun beat down on her head and burned into her cheeks and forehead. Ordinarily, she never stepped out the door without a layer of sunscreen on her face and one of her many protective hats perched over her expensively coiffed hair.

Today she didn't care. All she could think about was

Diana. She'd seen her daughter only a few days ago when she'd accompanied Thomas back to Dallas for a speaking engagement. And in spite of her bulging stomach, Diana had never looked more beautiful and radiant. The pregnancy was definitely agreeing with her.

Only two more weeks to go, less if the baby came early. That was always a possibility, and Anne wanted to make sure she was at the hospital when her grandchild was delivered. They'd all waited so long for this moment.

Which made it even more disturbing that she hadn't heard from Diana. Anne was sure that yesterday was her daughter's regularly scheduled trip to the doctor and Diana always called immediately to share the results. This time she hadn't.

Anne had tried to call Diana all last evening and again this morning. Diana either hadn't been home or hadn't answered the phone. Worse, she hadn't returned any of Anne's messages. She only hoped Diana wasn't avoiding talking to her because the doctor had discovered a problem with the pregnancy. Diana had wanted a child for so long, gone through so much to have Alex's child. She'd never be able to bear it if something happened to this baby now.

"Anne."

She turned at the sound of her name. Thomas was standing in the back door, shading his eyes with his hand and searching for her. A new wave of alarm skittered along her nerve endings. He'd been in San Antonio at the Mayor's Conference and wasn't due back until tomorrow.

"I'm over here, Thomas."

"What are you doing outside? It's too hot out here."

"It's still April."

"Since when does that matter in Austin?"

"I wasn't expecting you back until tomorrow," she said. "Is something wrong?"

"I'm afraid so." His voice was low and deep creases framed his eyes and marked his forehead.

Something foreign and bitter settled in the pit of Anne's stomach. "It's Diana, isn't it? It's the baby. I just know it."

"No. It's not the baby." He wrapped an arm about her shoulders. "But it is Diana."

"Is she hurt? Is she sick?"

"I don't know. I got a call this morning saying she'd been kidnapped."

Fear. Dread. Fury. They coalesced into a knot of ice that encased Anne's heart and choked away her breath. "Kidnapped." She repeated the word, but it seemed to come from someone else, someone who could still breathe and talk.

"It could have been a crank call, Anne. You know how often we get them these days. The world is full of nutcases, all convinced the government is out to get them. We just need to check it out."

"I've tried to call her for the past two days. She hasn't called back."

Thomas tried to hold her close, but she jerked away. Ever since he'd gone into politics, she'd worried that something like this would happen. All the time Diana had been growing up, she'd watched her like a mother bear would a troublesome cub, always fearful that one of the crazies who taunted her husband would take out his frustration on their daughter. Now the horror that had stalked her mind had become real.

But why now? Why when Thomas was riding the crest of popularity and Diana was only two weeks away from delivering her child? "Tell me everything, Thomas."

She listened while he gave her the facts. Too few. Too frightening. No ransom request. No hint of where Diana was being held. No mention of her return. Only the fact that Governor Thomas Kincaid had gone too far this time and Diana had been kidnapped in retaliation.

"What do they mean gone too far?" She was shaking, inside and out, and she fell against her husband's chest. "How could anyone be this cruel?"

"I don't know."

"I want her found, Thomas. Now."

"If she's been kidnapped, we'll find her quickly. I already have some of the best people in the business on this."

"I want more. I want you to call the police, the Texas Rangers, the FBI. Call in the National Guard and have them sweep every inch of land in the state if you have to, but *find my daughter*."

"*Our* daughter, Anne. And if I do as you say, this will become a media circus."

"Let it."

"No. I can conduct the search more effectively without interference from anyone. I know what I'm doing. Besides, the caller warned me not to bring in the authorities."

"Diana's my life, Thomas. The only thing I've ever loved besides you and I can't lose her."

He put a hand beneath her chin and tilted her head, forcing her to look into his eyes. "I know, sweetheart. I know. Do you think I love her any less?"

"No."

"Then trust me. I'll find her. Now, let's go back inside."

A couple of young men she didn't recognize were standing in the doorway when they reached the house. Thomas held her close for a few seconds, then left her side to go meet with them.

She walked past the strangers who were already deep in conversation with Thomas and went to the small study at the back of the mansion. Thomas had his ways. She had hers. In the silence of the room, she dropped to her knees and prayed.

DOC TURNED UP the empty bottle of whiskey, hoping for a last drop. All he got was the smell and a trickle of liquid, just enough to taunt him. Gritting his teeth, he tossed the bottle into the corner, wincing as it shattered into little pieces.

He glanced at Diana Kincaid. She was out so cold she didn't even jump at the sound of breaking glass. Lucky her. But he had no drugs and now he didn't even have a drop of whiskey to drown the demons that tormented him. And booze or drugs were the only way he could forget what he'd become part of. Men ruled by greed. Men who lived above the law, who considered no lives sacred but their own.

He paced the cabin, cursing, shaking. Conan had gone again, this time taking the infant with him and leaving Doc to guard Diana. He didn't know why the barbarian got to be the one to leave with the baby, the one who'd make the grand appearance and play the role of big shot while he got stuck in the middle of nowhere. It was always that way. He did the dirty work. Someone else got the glory.

His own fault, of course. If he hadn't lost out to the

booze and drugs, he'd be graduating from med school this year. Setting up his practice, seeing paying patients instead of jumping to the commands of a man who seldom even bothered to talk to him in person. Sure, they called him Doctor, but they didn't pay him like one, and they damn sure didn't treat him like one.

Still, the job paid for his drugs and his liquor. He needed a drink right now. Needed it bad, and he knew where he could find one. There was a bar back in the last town they'd driven through before turning off to come to the cabin. Not ten miles away. He could take the Dodge parked out front and be there and back before Diana opened her eyes from that last injection he'd given her, and probably long before Conan or one of the others came to take her off his hands.

He didn't know why he hadn't thought of it sooner, but now that he had, he saw no reason why he shouldn't go for the liquor. No one would be the wiser that he'd neglected his duties for a few minutes. Besides, he'd make sure Diana didn't go anywhere even if she did come to.

Using the sharp edge of his pocket knife, he stripped a length of fabric from the hem of the blanket that was tossed over her feet. He looped the band around her hands, knotted it and then tied it to the bedpost. That done, he stepped through the door and turned the key in the lock, just for a little extra insurance, though there was nothing to worry about. He'd be back before the woman in the bed even moved a muscle.

ROSS RACED THROUGH the maze of trees. His legs felt as heavy as the tree trunks that surrounded him, and every breath he took burned as if he were gulping in poisonous smoke. He hadn't heard footsteps behind him in a while, but that didn't mean the two lawmen weren't still on his trail or that they didn't have others looking for him now as well.

Still, it had been hours since he'd made the break, and he couldn't run much farther without stopping to get a second wind. He was in good shape. Working as a ranch hand the past year had done that for him, but he had his limits and if the pain in his chest was any indication, he'd probably passed those about three miles back.

He stopped and leaned against a towering pine tree while he tried to catch his breath. He hadn't noticed while he was running, but now that he'd stopped he could see a clearing up ahead, a patch of sunlight.

The change made him nervous. Clearings could mean people and people could mean trouble. He skulked through the trees, nice and easy, staying out of sight until he could see what waited in the clearing.

There was a small cabin set on the outer perimeter, but no sign of life. No old vehicles parked out back. No flowers growing around the steps. No weathered rockers swaying on the narrow porch. But there might be something he could use to help him get out of the damnable handcuffs. He waited and watched, still uneasy.

Finally, he took a step into the clearing, then pushed his body to jog the few yards to the cabin. He tried the doorknob. Locked tight. Glancing over his shoulder, he stepped to the window and peered inside.

Holding his hand up to cut the glare from the sun, he scanned the room. A small kitchen, a table, a couple of chairs and a—a woman.

He stepped away, shaking his head to clear it, but when he looked back, nothing had changed. A woman lay on the bed, a wild tangle of red hair framing her face. Her eyes were open, staring at him, coated by the same glaze he'd seen on addicts he'd arrested and hauled in for questioning back in the days when he'd been a detective on the Dallas Police Force. Her hands were tied and her face was pale. And the table by her bed was cluttered with used syringes.

He doubted anything inside the cabin would be worth dealing with the druggies who'd claimed the place first. Sick sex games played by depraved characters. It took all kinds. The woman looked as if she was well past the fun stages, if there had ever been any, but she wasn't his problem.

"Help me."

A pleading voice filtered through the cracks around the window seals. So weak, he thought he'd imagined it at first, but when he turned back to the window, he could see the redhead's mouth moving and read the desperation in her eyes.

"Help me. Please, help me."

He muttered a string of curses. Running for his life and now this. If he had any sense at all, he'd clear out and forget he'd ever come across this scene. He knew men who could have done just that. Unfortunately, he wasn't one of them.

He surveyed what he could see of the cabin, hoping he wasn't going to spy a couple of burly, *unhandcuffed* guys passed out on the floor. He didn't. The woman was the only sign of life.

His lungs still burned from the race through the woods, but he sucked in as much air as he could and heaved his left shoulder against the door. The half-rotted wood gave way in a spray of splinters and he pushed inside.

An extremely unwilling hero.

## Chapter Four

Diana stared at the man as he burst through the door. Scratches crisscrossed his face and arms, some painted with dried blood. Perspiration clung to his forehead and his hair fell into his face, half covering his dark eyes. His boots were scuffed, his jeans, worn and faded. But it was the handcuffs that captured her attention and made her blood run cold.

He stared at her, his muscles tense and straining against his cotton shirt. "Looks like we're in about the same shape," he said, his gaze leaving her to scan the room.

The relief she'd felt only minutes ago vanished. "You're a criminal!"

"No, I'm the prince and you're Snow White. All we're missing are the dwarfs and I imagine they're not too far behind."

"Who are you?" she asked, her tongue thick from the drugs. "How did you get here?"

He crossed the room, stopping at the head of her bed. "Look, lady, I didn't bust in here to give an interview. Do you want help or not?"

She nodded quickly, before he changed his mind and

bolted. "Please. Just cut the ties from my wrists so that I can get out of here."

"First things first. I need a promise that you'll do the same for me." He held up his hands.

She stared at him, anxiety rushing her senses, rattling her already strained nerves. Was she about to trade one hell for another, maybe for one even worse than she was in now?

He sauntered to the corner of the room and picked up a jagged-edged piece of a broken bottle. "I don't have all day, lady. Do we have a deal or not?"

"I can't break those cuffs." And even if she could, she wasn't sure she dared.

"I don't need you to break them, just help me unlock them. Right now, I'd say you're in no position to haggle."

"Do you have the key?"

"No. Guess the sheriff forgot to issue mine, but, we'll make do."

"If you escaped from the sheriff, why aren't you in a prison uniform?"

"Because I wasn't in prison. I was in a poor excuse for a county jail, and they didn't bother much with protocol." He stepped back to the bed and bent over her, the piece of glass gripped in his right hand.

She pulled away from him, though she couldn't move but a few inches before the ties cut into her wrists.

"Don't tell me you're afraid of me. I'm a pussycat compared to what you're used to." He slipped his hand beneath the knot of fabric that bound her to the headboard. "You might want to hold still, though. It's tough to cut when my wrists don't separate more than a few inches."

She held her breath as the glass sliced through the satin binding.

"You and your boyfriend must play some weird games."

The meaning of his comment sank in slowly, working its way through the haze of drugs. He thought she was here by choice, a tryst that had gone badly. That explained his attitude.

And she could tell why he might think that. Her clothes were strewn across a chair back and she was wearing a dingy white T-shirt that was too skimpy and had never belonged to her. The fragments of a broken whiskey bottle lay scattered among a couple of empties and a half-dozen used syringes rested on the table by her bed.

"I didn't come here with my boyfriend."

"Don't tell me you do this sort of thing for a living. It's a good way to get yourself killed."

"I've never..." She stopped herself from saying more. So he thought she was a slut. That was probably better than knowing the truth of who she was. If he found out that her father was the governor of Texas, he might be tempted to hold her for ransom himself.

"How long have you been in this place?" he asked, moving away from her and rummaging through the few groceries Doc and Conan had left on the homemade table.

"I'm not sure. About a week, I think."

"And now the party's over. Or did you just run out of booze and drugs?"

"I made a mistake," she said, determined to tell him no more than he needed to know. "Now I just want out of here. Quickly. Before the jerk I came here with comes back."

She managed to sit up straight in bed though the room seemed to shift and she had difficulty focusing. "Throw me my clothes, please," she said, anxious to make a run for safety while she still could.

He picked up the black skirt, and oversize white shirt and dropped them to the foot of the bed. If he noticed they were maternity clothes, he didn't mention it.

She held up the white shirt. "Now turn the other way while I get dressed."

"Yeah, I'm sure you're real modest, lady." But he turned and started digging around in the drawers that were in the cabinets in the kitchen section of the cabin. "Matches," he said, slipping a book of them into his pocket. "They might come in handy. And a pen. Looks like my luck is changing."

"I hope you're not planning to write your memoirs. The man who left me here could be back any moment."

"I have a little more living to do before I write my life's story. I'd like to come up with a better ending." He unscrewed the top of the pen and took the cartridge from the casing. Using the same piece of glass he'd used to free her, he sliced into it.

She wiggled and shrugged into her clothes. The skirt was too big. So was the shirt. The disparity was a cruel reminder that the baby she'd carried for nine months had finally left her womb only to be stolen from her. She swallowed hard, determined not to give in to grief. There was no time for pity. Alexandra needed her, and she had to keep her wits about her until she could get her daughter back.

"I'm ready," she said, fighting a sudden bout of nausea as she walked across the room. She touched a finger to her right earlobe, suddenly remembering that she'd had on a favorite pair of earrings when she'd been kidnapped. They were nowhere in sight now. Ross kept working on the stupid pen cartridge. "Are you making a weapon?"

"Not at the present, though that's not a half-bad idea. I need a thin edge of plastic to insert between the gears and the teeth of the lock. If I can get it to fit right it will work just like a key."

"You mean it's that easy to get out of handcuffs?"

"Not always. These are old and not quite as tamper-proof as the newer models. The links are thinner."

"Obviously you've done this before."

"I could say the same—" He turned, noticed she was dressed in maternity clothes and stopped in midsentence. "You're pregnant?"

"I *was* pregnant. The baby was born days ago. I'm not sure exactly how many, but I'd guess four or five."

He shook his head as if he couldn't comprehend what she was saying. His eyes bore into hers, scrutinizing. "What really went on in this cabin?"

"It's a long story, and we don't have time for it. Just show me how to unlock your cuffs. If we don't leave quickly, neither of us may get out of here alive."

ROSS SWALLOWED A CURSE. He had no idea what he'd stepped into, but the scenario he'd painted in his mind when he'd burst through the door a few minutes ago was fading fast. This wasn't just a sick rendezvous turned sour.

He stared into the woman's eyes. "Where's your baby?"

"Someone took her."

"Took her where?"

She glanced toward the door, her eyes glazed with fear. "I have no idea." Hands trembling, she took the thin sliver of hard plastic from his fingers. "Please, just tell me what to do. We have to hurry."

"I'm all for that." He held out his hands and gave instruction as to how to fit the roughly fashioned key into the groove. She worked slowly, her hands unsteady, her perfectly manicured nails, all except the two that were broken, sliding against the metal until she finally found the groove and loosened the catch.

Exhilaration rushed his senses as the cuffs fell loose. Strange how bonds degraded a man, stole his confidence and feelings of self-worth.

The lady yanked the cuffs from his wrists and dropped them to the floor. His foot was already in motion to kick them across the room when he thought better of it. "Never know when these might come in handy," he said, bending to retrieve them.

She backed away from him, and he realized she thought he might be about to use them on her. "You don't have to worry about me kidnapping you," he said. "I work alone." He walked to the table and grabbed an apple, a candy bar, a hunk of cheese and a couple of bottles of water. "You might want to take something to eat and drink as well," he said, stuffing the supplies into one of the plastic grocery bags that littered the table and then cinching the bag around his belt. "Unless you know a quick way out of these woods."

"I don't even know where we are. Are we still in Texas?"

"East Texas. Folks call this the Big Thicket. Lots of trees and wildlife. Not much else." And he was about to leave a woman to fend for herself. One who was pale and weak and unsteady on her feet. One who had just given birth to a baby who was nowhere around.

"Look, lady, I'd like to help you back to civilization.

I really would, but I'm not the guy you want to be hanging out with. I've got men with guns chasing after me, and they're not too choosy about who they shoot.''

''That's okay. I'll be fine.'' She grabbed a bottle of water and an apple from the counter, then went back for her pads and spare cotton panties that Doc had left on the table by the bed. The bleeding had almost stopped, but once she was up and moving it could start again. She stuffed everything into a plastic bag and slung it over her right shoulder. ''If you could just point me toward a highway.''

''Head east. You'll come to something.''

She staggered toward the door, holding on to a chair back and then to the wall, the drugs Doc had given her to keep her quiet stealing her equilibrium. A car engine droned in the distance. ''It's him,'' she whispered, the words more like a cry. ''We have to run.''

Only she couldn't, not in the condition she was in. And he couldn't leave her. He scooped her up into his arms and raced out the opening where the door had been and into the cover of the woods. He was back where he'd come from a few minutes ago, but now he'd exchanged the handcuffs for a woman. One with secrets of her own that he probably didn't want to know.

Alone, he might have escaped. Now he'd have a better shot at finding horse thieves in heaven than he'd have at getting out of these woods alive.

DIANA DRAGGED through the forest, forcing her body to keep up with the man who'd freed her from the cabin. They'd barely escaped the house in time, and the thud of a car door still echoed through her mind. It had probably been Doc returning from wherever he'd gone, and she could imagine him behind them, searching, ready to wrap his scrawny arms about her body and plunge another needle into her flesh. When she slowed, she could almost see his bloodshot eyes glaring at her through the shadows of the forest.

A mosquito buzzed about her ear. She swatted, hitting only air. The convict still marched in front of her, saying little, but slowing when she couldn't keep up and holding low branches and prickly shrub aside when they impeded her path. But in spite of his actions, the few comments he'd made had assured her that she was a liability to him, baggage he didn't want and couldn't afford. He was on the run, just as she was, but their enemies were vastly different.

Still, she needed him. Needed his knowledge of this pine forest that grew so thick it blocked the sunshine, allowing only shadows and dim light to penetrate it. Without his help, she'd walk in circles until she dropped. Then Doc and Conan would find her and carry her back to the never-ending nightmare.

Fear pitched in her stomach at the thought and she fought the resulting nausea with quick breaths. Before the abduction, her life had been sane, filled with anticipation. She'd been excitedly awaiting Alexandra's birth, putting the finishing touches on the nursery, packing a few necessities in the bag she'd planned to take to the hospital when the first pangs of labor hit.

Eagerly awaiting the birth of a child she'd wanted so desperately that she'd had her dead husband's preserved sperm implanted inside her. The fertility treatments had failed while Alex had been alive. But almost a year after his death, she'd finally gotten pregnant. And the knowledge that she'd be having Alex's child had done more than anything else to help her deal with the grief of losing him.

Now she was escaping through the woods with a criminal as her guide. And somewhere her precious baby girl was facing the world without her. Her eyes burned at the thought and a tear escaped and ran down her cheek. Using the back of her sleeve, she flicked it away. She couldn't show weakness.

The drugs were beginning to wear off. Some of the opaque haze had cleared from her mind, but her body still ached from the ordeal of the past few days. She stopped to catch her breath.

The man looked back at her and glared.

She braced herself against the trunk of a skinny pine tree.

"Is something the matter?" he asked.

"I just need a minute to catch my breath."

He ran his western hat back from his forehead. His face was bronzed from the sun and his features were craggy, rugged, like his voice. Still, he seemed far more human than the apes who'd kidnapped her, and he was her salvation for now.

"You go ahead," she said, bending over to rub a sudden cramp that gripped the muscles in her right calf. "I'll catch up."

But he didn't go ahead. Instead he walked back to stand beside her. If she hadn't known better, she'd have thought she detected a touch of compassion in his granite eyes. He took out the bottle of water he'd taken from the cabin, unscrewed the cap and handed it to her. "I guess having a baby is no picnic."

"Not the way I did it." She sipped the water, warm from the heat of the day and from riding next to the man's body, but still it felt good sliding across the scratchy dryness of her throat.

His gaze narrowed. "I'd like to know what happened back at that cabin."

She averted her gaze, not wanting to anger him, yet afraid of what he might do if he guessed her identity.

The man kicked at a clod of dirt. "I'm not trying to nose into your business, lady. But I run a lot smarter when I know what I'm up against. Is the man you're running from your pimp? A jilted boyfriend? A jealous husband?"

"No, of course not." She looked up and stared into his penetrating eyes. "No one I know would do something as sadistic as what I've been through."

"That's nice, but not exactly an explanation."

"If I tell you what happened, you probably won't believe it."

"Try me."

"Okay. I was abducted by a dark, muscular man. He took me to that cabin and turned me over to a couple of monsters. I went into labor early, probably as a result of being frightened half to death. As best as I can tell, that was about five days ago, maybe longer. It's difficult to know for sure with all the drugs they were pumping into me. This morning, at least I think it was this morning, the brute called Conan took my daughter and left."

He let out a low whistle and propped his foot on the stump beside her. "You're right," he said, "I have trouble buying that story."

She swallowed hard. She'd let his insinuations get to her, to prod her into saying more than she meant to. It was as if she could see the wheels turning in his head now. He was probably already planning how he could collect the ransom the goons back at the cabin would miss out on now that she'd escaped.

"You said we shouldn't stay here long," she said, anxious to end the conversation.

"We shouldn't. Drink a little more water. It will keep you from getting dehydrated."

She took a large swallow, then handed the bottle back to him. He turned it up, but took only a sip before replacing the cap and dropping it back into the bag. Saving it, she was sure, and yet he'd encouraged her to drink her fill.

"I'm trying to picture this scenario," he said, "but it's got more holes than a pound of Swiss cheese in a rat's nest."

"I can't help that. I've told you the truth."

"And you're sure you've never seen the perps before?"

"The perps?"

"Sorry, the kidnappers."

"All I know is that when I drove into my garage at my own home, a man was waiting for me. I didn't see him approach the car, but the second I stepped out, I was knocked to my feet and a blanket was thrown over my head. I tried to fight him off, but he was over six feet tall and extremely strong. He took me to the cabin and left me there." She hugged her arms around her chest and ground her feet into the carpet of pine straw.

"These men…" He stuck his hands deep in his pockets and stared at the toe of his boots. "Did they…hurt you? I mean— You know…?"

She knew. She read the concern in his eyes and for the first time she had the feeling he just might believe her. It helped, though she wasn't sure why it should matter what some escaped convict thought of her. "If you're asking if they raped me, the answer is no. If you're asking if I felt their slimy stares all over my body, if they managed to put their hands in all the wrong places, the answer is yes.''

The memories took over her mind, and she forced air into her lungs and then buried her face in her hands.

''I'm sorry.'' He waited until she looked up and met his gaze before he said more. ''I'd like to think that they'll get what they deserve before this is all over, but I wouldn't bet the ranch on it.''

''I can't worry about that right now. I just want my daughter back—safe. That's why I must get back to civilization and report this to the authorities. I appreciate that you're helping me do that.''

He backed away from her, his lips drawn tight. ''You have a short memory, lady. Those handcuffs you cut off of me earlier didn't get there by accident. The last place I'm going is to hunt up some cops.''

''Then don't take me to the cops. Just get me out of these woods and to safety. Quickly. I won't turn you in. I'll never even mention that I saw you.''

''And just where is it you think I can take you that's safe?''

''Into any town. I'll pay you well for your services.''

''I show my face in any town around here and the only thing I'll be able to do with that money is upgrade my casket.''

''If you're not taking me back to civilization, then where are you taking me?''

''I'm not *taking* you anywhere, ma'am. I helped you get out of the cabin and now you're following along of your own free will. The truth is, you're probably in the second most dangerous place you could be in right now. I've got a sheriff on my tail who plans to make sure that I don't see another sunrise. If you're with me, he'll

figure you're fair game as well. He's not a real discrim-
inating kind of fellow.''

"He won't shoot you if you give yourself up. He's
an officer of the law, not an executioner. He'll see that
you get fair treatment.''

"Yeah? What planet are you from?''

"This one, and I have connections. I can speak on
your behalf, get you a lawyer. What were the charges
against you?''

"Murder.''

He said the word almost tauntingly. The sound of it
lasered itself into her brain.

"So now you know the rest of the story,'' he said.
"Do you still want to hire me as your bodyguard?''

"Yes.'' The answer came out before she even
thought about it. But even if it hadn't, her response
would have been the same. ''I want my baby back.''

He studied her for long agonizing seconds. "Then I
guess you've just hired yourself a guide.'' He turned
and started to walk away. A few steps later, he stopped.
"I usually trade names with the person who hires me.
Mine's Ross Taylor.''

"I'm Diana.'' She didn't volunteer a last name. Fortunately he didn't ask, didn't seem to care that she
hadn't supplied one. She followed in silence, like a couple of hikers on an adventure in the great outdoors.

Only she was probably being stalked by a madman.
And her guide was an escaped prisoner, accused of murder. Things couldn't get much worse.

A second later she discovered how wrong she was.

# Chapter Five

Diana froze and listened. A rustle in the grass. A rattle, a baby's toy, or a maraca played by a light breeze. And then she caught a glimpse of the snake.

"Don't move, Diana. Stand very, very still."

Ross's voice slid along the edge of her terror, low, yet commanding. The rattlesnake uncoiled, stretching its neck toward her as its tongue darted in and out of its mouth. Beads of perspiration slid down her forehead and rolled along the flesh between her breasts. One more step and her foot would have landed square on the snake's back.

"Don't make a sound. Don't even tighten your muscles."

Good advice. Only every nerve in her body was already stretched to its limit and her muscles were bunched so tightly, it would probably take Houdini to unravel them. Without moving her head, she cut her eyes toward Ross. He was a couple of yards in front of her, standing motionless beside a clump of thorny brush.

"That's right. Look at me. Recite the Pledge of Allegiance in your mind. Say the alphabet. Name the men you've slept with. Just don't move."

She tried the first two options, but her mind refused to focus on anything but the snake. It had started to inch forward again, to slide along the pine-strewn earth on its belly, its body a series of diamond-shaped humps and curves that seemed to grow longer and more menacing with every passing second. Moving toward her.

"Easy does it, Diana. Don't spook him and he'll crawl right by."

Crawl right by or else bury his fangs in the flesh above the tops of her shoes. Her mouth grew dry, and she all but stopped breathing as the snake's belly brushed the toe of her shoe. The scream rattled in her throat, and she tried desperately to keep it inside her. It would be amazing if the snake didn't react to the sound of her heart pounding against the walls of her chest or sense the frigid chills racing through her veins.

"Don't look at the snake, Diana. Look at me. Look in my eyes."

She forced her gaze away from the poisonous reptile and stared at the man who was trying to save her life for the second time today. *His eyes. Concentrate on his eyes. Hazel with darker flecks. Warm. Deep.*

"That's right, Diana. Hang in here with me. It's almost done."

His voice was different from what it had been back at the cabin. Then it had been edgy, jagged, like the glass he'd used to slice through the satin that had bound her wrists. Now it was soothing. Smooth. Like the lemon filling her mother used to spread between the layers of buttery cake still warm from the oven.

Her lungs hurt now, from the tightness and the lack of air. But she forced herself to stare into the depths of Ross's eyes. Strange, he seemed closer than the distance that separated them. Closer even than when he'd been standing over her bed. The bond between them seemed unbroken, as if they were touching. As if something in his eyes held her.

The grass rustled again. She dropped her gaze and saw the snake, hurrying away, disappearing into a thick clump of brush near a semiclearing. Her breath escaped her body in a rush of air, and she felt as if her bones had thawed and turned liquid, no longer able to hold her steady.

Ross stepped to her side and took her in his arms. She clung to him, held on for dear life, not swayed by the fact that he was a criminal or that she didn't know him. Not caring. Not thinking. She just couldn't take anymore.

"It's okay. It's all over with. You handled it like a pro."

She tried to answer him, but her mouth seemed unable to form words. She bit her bottom lip, closed her eyes tightly, but still the tears escaped and rolled down her cheeks in unchecked torrents. It was as if all the horror and fear of the last few days had finally exploded, and all she could do was hold on to this stranger and cry.

He held her close and stroked her hair, rocking her to him. There was no threat in his touch, no overtones, just strength and comfort. Finally, her sobs subsided. She sniffled and wiped the heels of her hands against her eyes.

"Thank you. You probably saved my life. Again."

"My pleasure."

But he continued to hold her, and the situation grew awkward between them. She was suddenly aware that he'd been the only man to hold her in his arms in the long months since Alex's death. The only man who had seen her cry.

She pulled away. "How did you know what to do?" she asked, not really caring, but feeling the need to make an attempt at conversation that didn't center around the fact that she had spent the last few minutes in his arms.

"You learn about snakes fast on a Texas ranch. Of course, I usually have a gun on me when I'm fixing fence or punching cattle. I've never had to *talk* a lady through a rattler's visit before."

"Anyway, I appreciate your efforts."

"I just did the talking. You did the hard part. It's not easy standing dead still while a rattlesnake crawls over your shoe."

"No. Nothing seems easy anymore." She buried her hands in the pockets of her skirt and found a tissue she'd forgotten was there. Taking a corner between her thumb and index finger, she dabbed at her eyes.

"Are you up to walking a little farther?" he asked.

"Do I have a choice?"

"I doubt the man who was holding you hostage is going to come traipsing this deep into the forest looking for you. He's probably cleared out of the area altogether by now."

"You have a lot more confidence in that theory than I do."

"Even if I'm right about him, the sheriff and his deputy aren't going to go away without putting a bullet in me, not if there's any way they can avoid it."

"If you're innocent, give yourself up. You'll get a fair trial with a jury of your peers."

"No offense, but I like my odds better if I do this my way."

"But the system works. You just have to give it a chance."

"It may work for you. For poor cowboys like me, it sucks." He reached over and wiped a stray tear from her cheek. "Now, you can go with me, or not. Your choice."

"Go with you or stay out here with the rattlesnakes. No thanks."

"Then let's rock and roll. It'll be dark soon, and I'd like to put as much distance as I can between us and the men who are actually armed and dangerous."

She was as ready as she'd ever be for a night in the wilds with a man charged with murder, an escaped criminal who'd become her protector. Only who was protecting Alexandra tonight? Who would feed her and hold her in their arms when she cried? Who would love her?

She pushed forward. Kidnappers, snakes, criminals, sheriffs with guns. They could all come at her, but she'd still find a way to get her baby back.

TROY MAGEE TRAMPED through the woods, cursing every step of the way. He'd been warned how important this job was. It should have been simple enough, but his bumbling deputy had blown it. Now there would be all hell to pay unless Ross Taylor was found and disposed of—properly.

Barefoot straggled along behind him, making more noise than a herd of cattle heading out to pasture. "Looks like you could at least keep up, seeing as how you're the reason we're out here in the first place. If you hadn't screwed up we could be home eatin' supper now."

Barefoot grunted. "It wasn't none of my fault that

lunatic jumped me. He's a crazed killer, that's what he is. Darrell Arnold never had a chance against him and neither did I.''

"Well, you're gonna get another chance at him, 'cause we ain't goin' home till we make sure he's deader 'n an armadillo come face-to-face with an eighteen-wheeler.''

Barefoot stopped walking. "If you think I'm staying out in these woods after dark, you're crazy as a bullbat.''

"I proved that when I hired you on. But we *will* be out here—as long as it takes to find Ross Taylor and complete the job we were paid to do. Me and you, and at least a half dozen other gun toters.''

"You mean, we've got backup?''

"I mean this place is crawling with men, all looking for Taylor. He ain't got a chance of gettin' out of here alive. But we're the ones that lost him, and it would look a lot better for us if we finish what we started.''

"Job or no, I don't like being out in these woods at night, especially when there's thunder rumbling off to the east.''

"You're not afraid of a little rain are you?''

"I don't like storms. Besides there's snakes. Spiders and scorpions, too, and who knows what else.''

"A killer by the name of Ross Taylor, that's what else. And he's got a lot more to worry about than you do. He's likely looking at his last sunset right now.''

Magee slowed and looked to the west. The sun was setting, and the temperature was dropping. Fast, the way it did in East Texas in spring. The mosquitoes would be out in mass soon, along with the night creatures that scurried across the dry earth and rooted for food beneath the trunks of the towering trees.

He'd have to step careful, make sure he was the one setting the trap and not the man walking into it. He knew Ross Taylor's reputation, knew what he was capable of. Pity the person who walked up unsuspecting on Ross Taylor tonight.

Ross stood in the shadows of the trees and stared at the first piece of good luck he'd run into in days. They'd stumbled onto a dilapidated hunting cabin. Half the windows were boarded over, the steps had rotted away and the place leaned seriously to the left. It would never make the local travel guide, but it had a roof and a man on the run took what he could get.

He turned to make sure Diana was still behind him. She'd slowed down considerably during the last hour, and he wasn't sure how much farther she could make it before she collapsed completely. The birth of her baby and the drugs her captors had pumped into her veins had taken a serious toll on her energy level.

If he had only himself to think of he'd keep going now, move by the light of the moon without slowing down, but she'd have to rest. And, if the storm that had been brewing for the past hour or so ever hit, she'd need shelter.

Lightning struck again, this time firing straight down instead of zigzagging across the sky. A booming crash of thunder followed on its heels. Diana picked up her pace, and she was breathing in choppy gasps when she stepped to his side.

"That last bolt of lightning looked as if it were coming right at us."

"It was close." He nodded toward the shack. "Shall I book you a room?"

She looked up and saw it for the first time. Her mouth

drew into a serious frown. "I'm not sure we wouldn't be safer in the woods."

"But we wouldn't be dryer. Besides, it's just a step below your previous lodging."

"A big step. The cabin I was held captive in had doors and windows. This place looks as if it's been bombed and gutted. Only a few windows still have glass in them, and the way it's leaning, I doubt it will hold up to a strong wind."

"It's probably stood for years. I imagine it'll make one more night."

She clutched his arm, her fingernails digging into his flesh. "I can't stay here all night. I thought you understood. I have to find my baby, and there's no time to waste on sleep."

He felt her desperation deep in his gut and he hated that he had no magic solutions to offer her. Or maybe he just hated the fact that he'd let her down. "Tomorrow, first thing, we'll get out of here. I'll get you to someone who can help you."

"No. Tonight. Every minute counts."

Lightning cracked and burst the darkness into a spray of neon brightness. Thunder followed on its heels, a crashing, earthshaking explosion of power.

Ross took Diana's hand, and tugged her into the clearing toward the cabin just as the first driving drops of rain stung their flesh. Fortunately, she followed his lead. By the time they reached shelter, they were already drenched through to the skin.

Diana stopped just inside the doorway. A streak of lightning lit up the sky and outlined her silhouette against the backdrop of the storm's fury. The maternity clothes that had hung loose a minute ago stuck to her in damp folds, clinging to the curves of her body. Her fiery red curls fell straight, the water dripping from the saturated strands, sliding down her brow and rolling down her cheeks. He reached up to brush a clump of wet locks behind her ears.

Her skin was soft beneath his rough hands. She shivered and drew away, and he knew instinctively that it was the intimacy and not the cold that had made her shudder.

"You don't have to worry," he said. "I won't hurt you."

"I didn't think that you would."

But relief tinged her voice, and if he could have kicked himself in the rear, he would have done it. Attention from a stranger with a surge of hormones was the last thing she needed after what she'd been through.

He turned away from her, dug deep into his right front pocket until he found the packet of matches he'd taken from the cabin. He removed one and lit it. It flickered and died. He was definitely in rare form tonight. He couldn't even get a satisfying spark from a match.

But the next one cooperated, shooting a nice steady flame skyward. Using it for illumination, he made his way around the room, checking to see if there was anything they could use. The furnishings were sparse, an old iron bed with a set of busted springs and no mattress. A rocking chair with the seat rotted away. A wooden table.

Apparently they weren't the only people who'd sought shelter in the cabin. A stack of old blankets cluttered one of the back corners of the room, and a supply of squashed beer cans and their empty cardboard cartons were piled next to them.

Way back in the rear of the one-room structure was a pile of dry logs. "Looks like somebody up there might like us just a little.'' He walked over to the logs and nudged one of them with his foot. A Texas-size scorpion jumped out and scurried across the floor, its escape spotlighted by a poorly timed flash of lightning.

Diana jumped a foot into the air. ''Don't just stand there and let him get away. Kill him.''

''What happened to all that talk about justice and not killing without a fair trial?''

''It doesn't count for scorpions and snakes.''

''That's what the sheriff said. Only I think he included worthless cowboys in his version.'' He smashed the escaping creature beneath his boot just as the match burned down to flesh. He didn't bother to hold back the curse that jumped to his lips as he dropped the match to the floor and ground it beneath his boot.

Diana stepped close behind him. ''I don't see how you can joke about the fact that someone is trying to kill you,'' she said. ''Or about scorpions either, for that matter.''

''Would you like me better if I wailed and complained?''

''I don't like or dislike you, Mr. Taylor. I don't even know you.''

''That's obviously true. No one who knows me puts a Mr. in front of my name. An adjective or two maybe, but never a title.''

''Maybe you should get new friends.''

''An excellent idea. If I get out of this alive, I'll try to find a more genteel group of people to associate with. I don't guess you have any outcasts in your group you could throw my way.''

''Now you're making fun of me.''

''It's part of my charm.''

''Well, you can't hurt my feelings. Nonetheless, your

time would be better spent building a fire. That way we can keep warm and see if there are more scorpions lurking about and waiting to attack us.''

''Yes, ma'am. Anything you say, ma'am.'' He bowed in a show of mock servitude, but he couldn't help smiling. The woman was amazing. Snakes and scorpions sent her into fits of terror, but she seemed to take being abducted and then rescued by an escaped convict in her stride. She was obviously used to giving orders. Her husband was probably more henpecked than a dying rooster.

But, it was tough to feel too sorry for him. Even wet as a drowned rat, the woman had sex appeal to spare. She'd given him a rise a few minutes ago, and he was on the run for his life.

Her husband was probably going nuts since she'd disappeared. Not that she seemed too worried about him, or about herself either, for that matter. Her concern was all for her baby and, much as it surprised him, Ross found that damned endearing.

A blistering streak of lightning split the dark sky with a crack of bright light. The crash of thunder that followed shook the walls and floor of the cabin like a sonic boom.

Diana moved closer, so close he could feel her breath on the back of his neck. The feeling sent a jolt through his system that landed at a very susceptible body part. He stepped away, sure that had not been her intention. He made a mental note to add thunderstorms to the list of things that frightened her and to add Diana to the list of things that frightened him.

He bent and picked up a few logs, carried them over to the fireplace and stacked them on a rusted grate. Diana stooped down beside him and slid one of the beer cartons beneath the logs. "This should get a flame started."

"You look as if you've done this before," he said.

"Not under the same circumstances, but I've lit a few fires in my day."

"I don't doubt that for a second." Ross struck another of the precious matches and placed the flame beneath the ragged edge of the cardboard carton. The blaze caught and started licking its way around the dry logs.

Diana pulled the seatless rocker toward the fire.

"I don't think I'd try sitting in that," he said.

"I don't plan to." She fingered the top button of her soaked shirt. "We need to get out of these wet clothes before we catch pneumonia," she said. "We can hang them on the back of the rocker to dry."

He swallowed hard. "I don't think that's a very good idea."

"Look, Mr. Taylor—"

"Ross."

"Okay, Ross. I have to find my baby. I won't let you, the storm, those lunatics that stole her or a bout of chills and fever because I don't have sense enough to get out of these soaked clothes stop me. If you can't handle that, you'll just have to sleep outside in the storm."

He groaned as Diana loosed the second button. The shirt parted just enough to reveal a glimpse of bare flesh and a white, lacy bra before she turned away from him, but not before he realized his self-control was about to be seriously put to the test.

He'd stayed away from Texas as long as he could stand it, finally moving back a little less than a month ago. Now he had a murderous sheriff behind him and was about to have a sexy, naked new mother in front of him. A woman who was further off-limits than the Canadian border.

And he'd thought there would be no one to welcome him home.

# Chapter Six

The fire sputtered and popped as the flames licked their way along the logs. The flickering blaze gave the squalid room a surreal quality, a sense of warmth, of rightness, in a world that was dreadfully wrong. The heat seeped into Diana's bones, chasing away the chill.

She sat cross-legged, huddled in her blanket. The synthetic fabric felt surprisingly soft against her bare skin, and she clutched it tightly, swaddling it around her so that nothing below her neck was exposed to the penetrating eyes of Ross Taylor.

She'd tried to sound calm and authoritative when she'd announced that they had to get out of the wet clothes, but the idea of stripping naked in his presence had bothered her far more than she had let him know. It made her uncomfortable, but strangely elicited no fear.

Maybe that was because she'd already looked into the eyes of the devil himself in the past few days, the devil and his helpers, and she knew Ross was not anything like those men. Or possibly she'd just developed a false sense of trust when he'd guided her through the up-close-and-personal experience with the rattler.

Nonetheless, she'd felt a distinct rising of the tension

level when she'd wrapped herself in the blanket and
started wiggling out of the soaked clothes. The invisible
boundaries that separated them were fragile at best, and
she feared that one suggestive move on her part might
send him vaulting over the barriers. He was, after all,
not only a desperate criminal, but a man.

Still, if she'd stayed in the wet clothes, she'd have
surely become sick and even weaker than she was already. And weakness was not an option. She was on a
quest to save her daughter from the hands of a madman.

Ross picked up the plastic bag he'd fortunately had
the good sense to fill back at the abductors' cabin.
"Let's see," he said, peeking at the contents. "You can
have an apple, cheese or a candy bar. And to wash it
down, I can offer you a fine white water, bottled from
a pure spring, if the label can be believed."

"Actually, it's mostly your food. I only have a bottle
of water and an apple."

"Who's counting? Besides, the company of a beautiful woman is what makes a dinner party a party." He
broke off a hunk of the cheese and handed it to her. His
hand brushed hers as they made the exchange and an
uneasy awareness quaked inside her. She took the
cheese with a murmured thanks and avoided any eye
contact.

Lightning threw a blinding streak of illumination
across the sky, and the deafening rumble and crash of
thunder rattled the few remaining panes of glass in the
windows. She trembled at the fury and burrowed even
further inside her blanket.

"A lovely night for a picnic," Ross said.

"If you like a storm."

"I don't mind them. A good storm breaks the tension
and clears the air. Tonight it has an added bonus."

"What's that?"

"I'm alive and dry and the good sheriff who wants me dead is probably stamping around in the rain and mud, growling and cursing and growing more miserable by the minute."

She finished off her cheese and Ross pulled the apple from his bag and placed it in her hand. "Eat what you want," he said. "I'm a steak-and-potato man myself."

"I don't recall that being on the menu."

"Not unless we find someone who responds to smoke signals and delivers outside a thirty-mile radius."

"You don't really think we'll have to walk thirty more miles to get out of these woods do you?"

"No, though it might be better for me if I could manage to lose myself in them forever."

She bit into the apple. The fruit was crisp, and the flavor exploded in her mouth releasing a spray of juices that moistened her lips. She licked them clean but turned away when she saw Ross watching her. Stretching her legs toward the fire, she chewed the bite of apple slowly, savoring the taste, knowing that the little food they'd taken from the cabin wouldn't last long. "We'll share," she said, passing the apple back to him.

He took it reluctantly. "Funny, I feel a little like Adam when Eve offered him the forbidden fruit."

"I'm harmless."

"Are you, Diana?" He toyed with the apple before looking up to stare into her eyes. "You've already offered me a bargain I didn't have sense enough to refuse."

"All I asked for was your help as a guide."

"And you make it sound so simple. Just lead you into town. Turn you over to the same cops who probably have an APB out on me right now."

A hint of guilt attacked her conscience, but she pushed it aside. It wasn't herself she was fighting for now. It was Alexandra. "I told you that I don't need you to go to the cops with me. Just help me find a way out of these woods. Leave me on the side of the road somewhere or at a farmhouse where I can get help. That's all I ask."

"But if I abandon you before the job is finished, I won't be able to get the reward you've promised. So, you see, Diana, you're not harmless or helpless. You hold all the cards."

"So why are you taking the risk?"

"I'm a poor cowboy and the sheriff has the power of the state of Texas behind him. I'll need the money to get out of the area, disappear into the masses of some faraway metropolis before I'm taken into custody again."

The apple that had tasted so good going down turned to acid in her stomach. Ross Taylor, wanted for murder. She studied his profile in the glow from the fire. His edges were all rough, his skin bronzed from the sun. His nose was just a tad off-kilter, as if it might have been broken once. A strong jawline, a manly mouth.

The kind of image you used to see on billboards advertising cigarettes. Not the kind of man you'd think capable of murder. Yet, she'd read once that anyone was capable of murder if the situation was right.

At the time, she'd been sure that nothing could ever enrage her so that she'd be capable of taking a life. Now she knew differently. She could have easily killed Conan when he'd started out the door with Alexandra. All she'd needed was the strength and a weapon. Maybe it had been like that for Ross Taylor.

He stood and poked at the blaze with the end of a

log. The fire sputtered, then shot up, throwing a flash of heat into her face. "Did you really kill a man?"

The question came out before she'd had a chance to think about it. Now she wished she hadn't asked. His face twisted into a scowl and his body grew hard, his eyes dark and threatening in the glimmer of firelight.

He stared into the fire. "It doesn't seem to matter if I killed a man or not. Someone believes I did, and that someone has the power to try and convict me without the trappings of a courtroom or a judge. I've been sentenced as well, only I escaped before the sheriff had a chance to perform the execution."

"Why were you out in the woods with the sheriff instead of behind bars?"

"Another prisoner and I were supposedly being transferred to a different jail, one where the security was tight enough to keep me from escaping and keep the irate townspeople from breaking inside to take care of me themselves. I had trouble believing that scenario from the get-go."

"But that's not unheard of."

"No, but then the sheriff and his deputy came up with some bull about how the engine sounded funny. Fortunately, I knew enough about cars to know that was a crock. Once we'd stopped in the middle of nowhere, it was clear that either I or the other prisoner was going down."

"So you managed to escape?"

"I made my move. Used the deputy who was along for the ride as a shield until I backed to the edge of the woods and made a run for it."

"What about the other prisoner?"

"He didn't play quite as smart. He took off running

while still in the open. A bullet to the brain stopped him."

"But he was killed while trying to escape. That's not the same as shooting a man in cold blood without reason. Maybe you misread the situation and there really was something wrong with the car's engine."

"Sorry, lady. All that justice crap you preach sounds real good, but it doesn't fly over the chicken coop. I'm on someone's hit list. Maybe because they really believe I killed Darrell Arnold. Maybe because they don't like the way I look or the way I wear my hat. Some people don't need a lot of reason to want you dead."

"Then you didn't kill Darrell Arnold?"

He sat down on the floor beside her and stretched his legs in front of him. "Not that I remember."

Anxiety raised the hairs on her neck. "I would think you'd know if you'd killed a man."

"Yeah, you'd think so."

"I don't understand. What are you saying? You're surely not claiming to have amnesia."

"Not hardly. My memory's fine. Believe it or not, but my head is not quite hard enough."

"I'm not following you."

"I was sitting in some no-name bar having a drink and minding my own business. A fight broke out. Someone threw a punch my way. I threw a couple back and the next thing I remember, something crashed against my skull."

"If someone knocked you out, you could hardly have pulled a gun."

"That was my story. The sheriff didn't agree."

"But there were people around. Witnesses."

"Funny thing about witnesses. They always manage to see the facts that can hurt you and never the ones

that can help. Everyone saw me throw a punch or two.
A few even saw me take the blow that knocked me
out.'' He rubbed his hand along a spot over his right
temple. ''But no one seems to remember seeing me
come to and leave the bar.''

''Maybe someone helped you to your vehicle.''

''All I know is that I came to in my truck, miles down
the road, with no clue as to how I got there. Next thing
I know I'm in some podunk Texas jail charged with the
murder of a man I barely knew.''

''But you did know him?''

''I did some work for him.''

''And you claimed my story was bizarre.''

''Believe what you choose. Everyone else did.''

He made it sound a lot simpler than it was. She'd
love to buy his story. That would make him just a cowboy who happened to be in the wrong bar on the wrong
night. An innocent person running for his life, the same
as she was.

If she didn't believe him, then she was alone in the
middle of a forest with a man who'd committed murder,
came up with a far-fetched alibi that didn't work, then
escaped from the law.

Either way, she'd have to be very careful, make sure
she didn't say anything to give away the fact that she
was Thomas Kincaid's daughter. Governor of Texas, a
man of power, of position, of wealth. A man who would
pay dearly for the safe return of his daughter. She
wasn't actually afraid of this man but she could well
imagine that he would be tempted to hold her for ransom, and she had no time for additional complications.

For all she knew, her father might have already paid
the ransom to the other men and still the slime had held
her prisoner and stolen her baby. But she was certain

her father didn't just pay the money and leave it at that. He would be conducting his own search by now, running it his way, leaving no stone unturned.

Still he'd be sick with worry. So would her mother. She had to find a way to call them, to let them know she was all right, at least she was all right unless the lunatics she'd escaped from found her again.

Or unless Ross Taylor actually was a cold-blooded murderer who was just waiting for the right time to slit her throat. The possibility seemed so far removed that it didn't even increase her heart rate. In fact, she was exhausted and warm and beginning to relax for the first time since she'd been pirated away from her home.

Ross stretched and paced the room, his blanket dragging the floor as he walked from one window to the next, staring out into the intensity of the storm as the rain pelted the glass with sheets of water. "You should try to get some sleep," he said, without turning to look at her.

"What about you?"

"I'll keep watch."

"You can't stay awake all night."

"One of us has to unless we want to risk a surprise visit. And you look as if you need sleep a lot more than I do."

She couldn't argue that point. Her sides and legs ached from the trek through the woods only days after giving birth to Alexandra. Now she had new appreciation for the pioneer women of old who'd gotten up from the birthing bed and gone straight to their regular chores.

"Do you promise you'll wake me when the storm lets up and we can travel again?" she asked, determined not to waste any more time than necessary.

"Count on it." He rolled a third blanket into a pillow and placed it on the floor next to her.

Clutching the blanket that covered her, she lay back and slid the makeshift pillow under her head. In minutes, the smell of burning wood and the song of the crackling fire lulled her into a zone somewhere between wakefulness and sleep.

Her mind drifted, played tricks on her. She was holding her baby girl, examining the tiny fingers and toes. Touching her velvety skin. Looking into her bright eyes.

An ache started in Diana's heart, then traveled down her arms. She folded them as if to cradle Alexandra to her chest, but all she felt was an emptiness that reached clear to her soul.

ROSS STARED OUT the window and into the pale grayness of the first sight of dawn. It was still raining. He could hear the pattering of drops against the roof and see them splatter against the window. They caught the glow of the fire as they danced down the dingy pane, joining up with other drops before pooling along the ridge of rotting wood at the bottom of the window.

Swelling, picking up speed. The way trouble did.

He should have never come back to Texas. He'd known that even when the urge to return had grown so strong he could no longer fight it. Texas had been his home, where his memories lived, where his life had begun.

And where it had fallen apart.

But it hadn't been Texas's fault. The blame all lay with a man. J. B. Crowe. The kingpin of the Texas mafia.

But this time Ross couldn't even blame Crowe for what had happened to him in Halpern. At least, it wasn't likely Crowe was behind Darrell Arnold's murder and Ross being framed for the deed, though nothing was beyond the man.

Crouching by the fire, he let his mind wander back to the other night in the bar. He hadn't told Diana everything. If he had, it would have given her more reason to fear him, and she was juggling enough problems without adding that to the mix.

He'd gone to the bar to confront Darrell Arnold. The man had cheated him out of a week's wages and, little though the amount was, Ross didn't like being cheated. Still, he'd already said his piece long before that fight broke out. And even if he'd thought Darrell Arnold was behind his getting clobbered, there was no way he'd have come to and gone searching for revenge with a loaded gun.

Not that he hadn't killed before. He had. One time too few. But if he was going to shoot a man down for wronging him, Darrell Arnold would not have been that man.

## DAY 6

IT WAS DAWN by the time the storm lost its fury, settling into a drizzle that might linger until well past sunup. But a few drops of rain would not stop the sheriff and his deputy and whatever posse he'd called in to help with the search. So, it was time for Ross to move on and leave sleeping beauty for another prince to find.

Reaching over, he felt the jeans that hung from the back of the rocker. Only the thick layers of fabric around the waist and the fly were still damp, and he could live with that. He let the blanket drop to the dusty floor.

Diana stirred beside him. He stood in his shorts, looking down at her. She was sexy as all get out wrapped in that blanket. Her long lashes feathered her flesh and the fiery red hair made her delicate features come alive. The color matched her determination. Bold. Brazen.

And off-limits, at least under the present circumstances.

He turned away and reached for his jeans. It was time for him to hit the road, and Diana would be better for his walking out of her life. He'd call for help the first opportunity he got. Send someone who could offer her more than the kind of trouble he courted. She'd need all the help she could get to find her daughter.

And right now he didn't even want to think of the type of psychos who would take an innocent baby away from its mother. If he wasn't in muck all the way to his eyeballs, he'd have liked to stick around and have a go at finding them himself. But as it was, he had nothing to offer Diana but more danger.

Moving soundlessly so as not to wake her, he finished dressing and stepped to the door. She threw her body from one side to the other as the door squeaked open.

"Alex. Alex, please. I need you."

The cry slipped from her lips. Alex. Her husband, of course. The father of the baby that had been stolen from her.

*Hang on, Diana. I'll make damn sure that Alex knows where you are.*

The woods were anything but silent as he left the clearing and made his way into the forest of pines and cedars and an occasional sweet gum or oak tree. Early birds called from over his head. A frog croaked in the distance. A rush of wings sounded overhead as an owl headed home after a night of hunting.

And the high-pitched yapping of dogs somewhere in

the distance. Possibly the sheriff, chasing him down with a pack of bloodhounds. If that were the case, he'd left the cabin just in time, made it back into the woods where he had a chance of escape.

And he wouldn't have to worry about finding help for Diana. The sheriff and his deputy would see that she was returned to safety. He hurried his pace, moving north now, not sure where he was or where he was going. He moved much faster without an injured woman at his heel.

Still, she stayed on his mind.

CONAN DISMOUNTED and tied his roan to a low branch of a tree, glad he'd decided to hunt by horse and not by foot. He'd covered a lot more ground this way and done it without sloshing through the mud, though he hadn't stayed dry.

He stared straight ahead at the rickety shack that stood a few yards in front of him. By rights it should have been blown away in a Texas tornado years ago. But a stream of smoke curled and swayed out the chimney, carrying with it the scent of burning wood. Someone had gone inside to take refuge from the storm. And that could mean that he'd found Diana Kincaid.

His pulse quickened. His mouth grew moist, his movements jerky as the possibility of success rocked though his senses. He walked across the clearing, not stopping until his foot landed firmly on the first step. Then he paused only long enough to pull his pistol from the holster before he eased the door open and peered inside.

DIANA JERKED AWAKE. At first she was only aware of the blast of cold air that had slammed against her face.

Slowly, she realized where she was and why. She shifted beneath the covers, then pulled them tighter. The front door was cracked open, letting in a draft. But the storm was gone and the blackness had softened to a gray haze shrouded in mist.

She pushed up to her elbows, still clutching the cover about her neck. "Ross. Are you here? It's time to get started."

There was no answer, but she heard the soft whoosh of someone's breath behind her.

"I'm not Ross. But you're right. It is time to go."

The familiar voice cut into her, like a knife plunged into soft flesh. The devil had found her again.

# Chapter Seven

Diana went weak. She couldn't think, couldn't move. This absolutely could not be happening to her again. Only it was. The truth rushed her senses with near crippling force.

She scanned the room and the bitter truth hit hard. Ross's clothes were gone. His promise to stay with her and help had been no more than a convenient lie.

Finally her gaze locked with Conan's. "Where did you take Alexandra?" she demanded, as if she had any power to make a demand.

"It doesn't matter what I did with the little squalling brat. You'll never see her again." He walked over and stood in front of the fire, turning to warm his backside, as if this were some cozy meeting and she was about to serve tea.

Shifting, she watched his movements, hating her vulnerability, despising the fact that she was on the floor, clad only in the blanket and her undies, staring up into the cold black eyes of this monster. "If you've hurt my daughter, I'll…" The threat died on her tongue as she watched his mouth curl into a taunting smile.

"You'll do what? Tell your *daddy* on me? Sorry, sweetheart, but I'm not afraid of Thomas Kincaid."

"My father will never pay you a penny if you've hurt Alexandra. And he won't pay if you hurt me."

The man threw back his head and laughed as if she'd just told a hilarious joke. "Is that what you think this is about, Diana? Money?"

"If this isn't about money, what is it about?"

"You disappoint me. I would have thought you'd have figured it all out by now unless you've been living in a bubble the last few weeks. Not that we won't get a nice sum for selling your baby on the black market, but that's just a little extra. The real reward is knowing Thomas Kincaid has been bested at his own game."

Diana tried to make sense of what the man was saying. He wasn't holding her for ransom, yet somehow this had to do with her father. Only he was suddenly admitting too much, which meant he had no intention of letting her get out of this alive. She had to think quickly. Time was running out.

Turning slowly, he surveyed the room. "Lucky for you that you happened upon this warm, dry place to wait for me. Of course, it wasn't nice at all for you to run out the way you did."

She did a visual measure of the distance between her and the door. If she was dressed—if she was on her feet already, she might be able to make a run for it, but she was lying down and the few moments it would take to stand would give him time to position himself to stop her from bolting. She rose to a sitting position, hugging her blanket close.

His gaze settled on her white shirt and black skirt that were stretched across the arms of the old rocker. "Looks like your clothes are all hung out to dry. Does that mean you're wearing only a smile and a blanket?"

Her skin crawled as his gaze slid across her like

slime. He smiled suggestively, as if he could see right through the opaque fabric. She felt dirty, soiled by a filth that ran far deeper than the dirt she'd picked up in the woods.

"Why are you doing this to me?" she asked, unsuccessfully fighting the desperation that churned inside her. "Why won't you give me back my baby and let me go home?"

"Your baby. That's all you think about, isn't it? You wonder if she's alive, if she's in pain. But you can save the worry for yourself. Your baby has a new mother, the only one she'll ever know."

"You'll rot in hell for this." She spit out the words, no longer able to hold her tongue. The man would do what he wanted with her anyway.

"I'll rot in hell for lots of reasons. Until I do, I plan to have myself a real good time." He bent, picked up a log and tossed it atop the dying fire. A shower of sparks flew from the grate and sailed to the floor around the brick hearth.

"Tell me where you took my daughter and I'll make certain you get more money than you could possibly get for selling her to someone else."

"You have no daughter, Diana. Not anymore. You may as well accept that." He smiled smugly. "Get your clothes on. Or not. It makes no difference to me. Either way, we're getting out of here."

"You won't get away with this."

"And who's going to stop me? Our illustrious governor?" He reached deep in his pocket and pulled out a pocketknife, opening it and sliding his thumb and index finger along the blade as he walked toward her.

Adrenaline shot through her in a suffocating wave. She rolled toward the door, but he was too quick for her. He grabbed her by the hair at her nape and yanked her toward him. Her eyes watered from the pain, but still she swung her arms and managed to land one blow across his face.

He slid the knife along her cheekbone before slicing through a clump of her hair. "A souvenir," he said, pushing her back toward the floor. "A clump of beautiful red hair from the head of the governor's daughter. Now get dressed before I decide that's all I take out of here."

Get dressed and go with him or stay here in the form of a corpse. Only even if she went with him, she'd probably still end up a corpse. But later was better than now. At least it would give her a chance to escape again. Still clutching the blanket, she gathered her clothes.

The bottle of water she'd brought from the cabin sat on the floor near the rocker. The wrapped candy bar and a chunk of cheese lay beside it. All that remained of the picnic she'd shared with Ross Taylor. The man himself had left without her, sealed her fate, made it almost impossible that she would be able to find her baby girl before it was too late.

She wished the sheriff who was after Ross Taylor godspeed.

ROSS'S BOOTS SANK into the mud, and his mind echoed the rhythm of the *slosh-suck, slosh-suck,* that sounded with each footfall. He should be running through the woods now, but he'd slowed his pace, his mind consumed with the image of the woman he'd left asleep by the fire.

When he'd walked out the door, he'd been certain that leaving her in the cabin was the best thing he could do for her. Now he was waffling. He couldn't imagine that the man she'd run from could have tracked them by himself. And even if the one who'd taken her baby had returned to help in the search, the two of them would have surely cut bait and run by now. They'd have wanted to clear out before she found her way back to civilization and had the woods crawling with cops looking for them.

The abductors had every reason to run, except that Diana could identify them. Or perhaps they were desperate for the ransom they thought she'd bring.

And none of that was his concern. She hadn't even told him her last name. He'd move twice as fast without her to watch over. He'd already done more than most men in his place would have done. All perfectly good reasons for him to keep moving. If he had any sense at all, he'd shove the woman totally out of his mind.

The whinnying of a horse interrupted his internal debate. Someone else was in the woods with them. Without stopping to think, he raced through the woods and back to the cabin.

Ross LOCATED the animal. A dark roan, saddled and tied to a low-hanging branch, out of sight of the cabin. There was no one in sight, which meant the rider was likely inside with Diana. She hadn't mentioned the kidnappers having a horse, but then they'd had almost twenty-four hours to get one, and hunting for someone on horseback in the woods made a lot more sense than doing it on foot.

He couldn't be sure that the man who'd ridden up on the horse was after Diana, but he doubted it was Sheriff Magee. The scoundrel had been brave enough as long as Ross had been handcuffed and he and the deputy had both wielded a loaded gun, but Ross couldn't see him poking around in the wilderness without backup.

But Diana had been missing for several days. Maybe the man with her now was part of a rescue team combing the area on horseback. In which case, Ross was definitely not needed.

A nice thought, but the apprehension that had sent him back to Diana didn't let up. He eased closer, one step at a time, until he was in position to study the shadows that occasionally darkened the windows. With only the firelight to back them, they were more form than detail, but after a few minutes he made out a man's face peering through the window.

He watched a while longer, but Diana was nowhere in sight. He rubbed a hand up the back of his neck, massaging tendons so tight and extended they ran like ribbons of steel beneath his fingers. He'd feel a lot more comfortable about this whole situation if he had a gun, but unfortunately they didn't grow on trees. So he'd have to settle for something that did.

The forest floor was littered with twigs and dead branches that had broken off and fallen during the storm. He chose one as large and solid as a club. At close range it would work just fine. At a distance, it was worthless.

He made his way back to the area where the horse was tethered. If he found out Diana was safe, he could mount him and ride away. If the man inside was the kidnapper, his best bet was to send the horse running, then sneak inside and take on the man, one on one.

The problem was, there might not be time to wait around for a sign. He was a hairbreadth away from loosening the rope when the front door squeaked open. He stepped behind a tree and waited.

Diana literally fell out the door, or else she was pushed. Her feet slipped in the mud and she barely managed to steady herself as a giant of a man stepped through the door behind her. This had to be one of her kidnappers.

The brute grabbed her arm. She yelped in pain. Fury shot through Ross, like a billiard ball leaving a cue stick. His grip tightened on the club in his hands and he longed to land it upside the man's skull. Diana had been right all along. The men who'd kidnapped her were desperate or crazy. Or both.

"You'll pay for this," Diana said, staggering in front of the man.

Conan shoved her again and this time Ross caught sight of the pistol aimed at Diana's head.

"I've been missing for days," she said. "Every lawman in the state will be looking for me by now."

"Funny I don't see them around here anywhere. Now shut up and walk. Neither of us would be stuck out here in this mosquito-infested jungle if you hadn't bolted while Doc fed his habit. Not that he'll be feeding anything anymore."

"What happened to him?"

"What should have happened a long time ago. A man with a monkey on his back's not worth the price of his flesh at a fish market."

Ross knew he had to wait until the last possible second to make his move. If he charged them in the open, he'd likely get shot. He'd have to be patient, take them by surprise.

Old habits took over, and as the seconds ticked away, he moved into the zone he'd always thrived on, where wits had to be razor sharp, and the slightest hesitation could cost you your life.

The man made it easy. He stepped around the horse, so close Ross could smell the perspiration embedded in his clothes and the cloying odor of insect repellent that clung to his skin. He hoisted the clublike branch over his head and brought it down on the man's back.

The man sank to the ground with a groan, but he didn't lose the gun. Rolling away from Ross, he aimed at Diana and pulled the trigger just as she jerked behind the trunk of a towering pine. The bullet ricocheted off the trunk, missing her by inches.

Ross kicked at the man's hand, and his boot collided with the fingers clutching the trigger. The gun flew into the air, somersaulting its way to a puddle of water and mud.

Ross dived for the weapon, expecting Diana's abductor to do the same. But the man jumped to the horse's back and took off, the hooves kicking a muddy spray over Diana. Ross fished the gun out of the muck and aimed, but the mechanism was clogged with layers of mud. The man and the horse disappeared into the army of trees.

"You came back."

"Yeah." Ross turned back to face Diana. The sun had broken the horizon now, and the first rays painted her hair in shades of strawberries and the blush wine his mother used to drink on hot afternoons. He felt a tightening inside him that seemed to cut off his breath.

"Why, Ross? Why did you come back?"

He fought the sudden impulse to hold her close while his mind wrestled with her question. He couldn't explain why he'd come back, didn't understand it himself. All he knew was that he was glad he had and even happier that he'd been in time.

"Maybe I just decided I'd have a better chance of

beating the odds against me if I had the reward you promised in my back pocket,'' he lied, swallowing hard in an attempt not to let the unfamiliar feelings show through.

She fell against him and he felt the shudder that shook her body. His arm went around her, and the softness of her felt strange against the roughness of him.

"Thanks," she whispered. "No matter why you came back, I definitely owe you one."

"One day I just might collect." Only he wouldn't, at least not the way he'd like to collect. He'd have no right. His fingers skimmed the flesh at the back of her neck and he felt the blunt edges where her hair had been sheared. His gut rolled sickeningly at the thought of the man taking a souvenir of his victim. That as much as anything told Ross what kind of man they were dealing with.

He dropped his arm from around her and stepped away.

It was neither the place nor the time for the feelings that rumbled through his body. Especially when they were stirred by another man's wife.

"We need to get moving," he said, his voice gruff from the strain his thoughts had produced. "You need a cop. I need a break. And we're both overdue."

DIANA TRAMPED behind Ross, following him just as she had the day before with still no sight of a road or a farmhouse. She slapped at a persistent mosquito that buzzed her ear. "Amazing. I finally killed one of the nasty creatures."

"Great, that only leaves a few million more."

Her foot tangled with a vine and she went catapulting

over a fallen branch. Ross turned just in time to catch
her before she went face first into the mud.

She clung to him while she steadied herself. "Looks
like I owe you again."

"Don't worry. I'm keeping score."

"I don't know how you keep your sense of humor
in spite of all you've been through, Ross Taylor. It's—
it's disgusting, that's what it is."

"Naw. It's just that you're used to more luxuries than
I am. A cowboy learns fast to make do with whatever
the gods and nature hand him."

"But even cowboys aren't usually running through
the woods."

"No, but we're frequently up until morning helping
to birth a contrary calf or out in bad weather from dawn
till dusk making sure none of them are trapped in a bog.
And it's definitely not unusual to be out in the rain
searching for a few that wandered through a downed
fence and onto the highway."

"Then I'm thankful I'm not a cowboy."

"There are worse jobs. I've had a few of them."

She gulped in another helping of air. "I'm ready to
walk now," she said. "And this time I'll try to stay in
an upright position."

"You won't have to worry about that much longer."

"Why?"

"We should reach a road in another ten minutes or
so."

She turned slowly, scanning every direction. "I don't
see a road. Now I suppose you're going to tell me that
cowboys can sense the nearness of concrete or asphalt."

"Absolutely. It clogs our lungs and causes an allergic
reaction. Why, I've known some cowboys who had to
be hospitalized after spending a night in Dallas."

She shook her head. "You're full of bull."

"True, but you're smiling. It looks good on you."

"It goes with the mud, blood and butchered hair."

"You underestimate yourself. You don't look half bad."

Diana started to comment, but the words never came out. She was stopped by the look in Ross's eyes. The compliment, such as it was, was probably a big concession for a man like him. Her cheeks burned, and an unexpected warmth settled near her heart. She pushed the feeling away, not willing to deal with any emotion now except the need to get out of these woods and find her baby. Especially not willing to deal with some ridiculous shred of attraction for a man just because he'd saved her life. Several times.

"The road's to the east of us," Ross said. "I heard a truck in the distance just before you fell."

"I didn't hear anything that sounded like traffic." She stood quietly and listened for a few seconds. "I still don't."

"Then you'll just have to take my word for it. When we reach the highway you can wave down a car and get them to drive you into town."

"What about you?"

"I think it's best if we part company here."

"What about your reward?"

"I'll pass on that this time. But if you want to repay me, think nice thoughts of me occasionally and don't mention to anyone that I was with you. I'm hoping the authorities think I've caught a ride and cleared the state by now."

"Of course." It made sense, so why was her anxiety level climbing at the thought of Ross leaving her on her own? He was wanted for murder, not the kind of companion most women would want.

"You'll be all right, Diana. You don't need me anymore." He reached over and took her hands in his, as if he could read her mind, sense her uneasiness at the prospect of being alone.

But it was more than being alone. It was what the brute had said to her in the shack this morning. It was the knowledge that this had more to do with her father than it did with her. It was the possibility that her baby might have been sold like a sack of potatoes.

"I'm not going to the cops." The statement slipped from her lips even before she'd realized that she'd made that decision.

"What are you talking about?"

"I have to find Alexandra, and I can't trust the cops in this. If they get involved, if this hits the newspapers, I'll never see her again. Don't ask me how I know that. I just do." Her voice was shaking, but she knew without a doubt what she had to do.

"You've been through a lot, Diana. You're tired and you're not thinking straight. You need to go home. Let your husband and your family take over."

"There is no husband."

"But the baby's daddy?"

"He's dead, Ross. I'm alone in this. Look, I can't go into all of the gritty details now, but the man who found me this morning was the one called Conan. He was the same man who took my baby away. Only this morning, he said something...." Her voice trailed off, lost in the plan that was taking shape in her mind. "I can't go to the police, and I can't go home. Not yet."

Ross thrust his hands into his front pockets and stared at her, his eyes mirroring a concern that surprised her.

"You're not making sense, Diana. What did the man say that makes you think you can't trust the police or even your own family?"

"It's not that I can't trust them." She shoved her hair back from her face with both hands, letting her fingers tangle in the disheveled mass. "I need your help. Just for a few days, until we can find Alexandra."

He shook his head. "I'm not your man, Diana. I don't know who you are. You don't know me."

"You saved my life. You came back when you didn't have to. And it wasn't for the money. If it had been, you wouldn't be ready to send me on my way now."

"I'm an escaped murder suspect."

"You're innocent. I'd stake my life on it."

"You are."

"I know, but I'm not afraid. Not of you."

"That's great. You're not afraid, but I am."

"You don't need to be. I'll hire you the best lawyer money can buy, and he'll prove your innocence. I can afford it. Trust me."

"Trust you? I've tried that before. With women and with men. I got burned every time."

He touched a rough hand to her cheek, and she felt a slow, heated need shimmy up her spine. She hadn't been with a man since her husband had died. Hadn't wanted to. So, why now, when she'd been through so much, when her heart and mind were centered on getting Alexandra back, did she tremble at this stranger's touch?

"You need someone who understands what you're up against," he said. "Someone who has the power of a badge behind them."

"I need someone who's brave and smart and who finds a way to get things done. That's you."

"No, I'm a loser. All the way. Besides—" He kicked at a clump of mud beneath his feet "—I'm a man, Diana. You're a woman. If I'd just met you on the street, it might work. But I've heard your soft breathing while you slept, watched your breasts rise and fall while you lay naked beneath a blanket. A man can only take so much."

"I need your help, Ross. I'll take my chances with everything else."

He shook his head and stepped away. "What is it you think I can do?"

"I don't know what it will take, but I have to find my baby. Don't desert me in this, Ross. Right now you're the only game in town."

"So that explains how I beat out the competition."

But he released his breath in a huff of air and she knew she'd won. They walked on, this time in silence, trudging through the mud and swatting at mosquitoes and gnats and wiping spiderwebs from their hair and faces. A few minutes later, they came to a rutted path that vaguely resembled a road. "I hope this isn't the highway you were talking about."

"No. This is just an old logging road, but it probably connects to the highway."

"Then we can just follow it."

"Not a good idea. I prefer the covering of trees when I have men looking for me."

"As long as—"

"Wait." He held up a hand to quiet her.

A car was coming, cutting through the woods not twenty yards from where they were standing. Ross grabbed her arm and pulled her behind a cluster of brush.

"Keep still and don't make a sound."

She did. The car was actually a mud-splattered, dirt-brown Jeep Wrangler with oversize tires that gave it the appearance of a lunar-landing vehicle. It stopped and a blond boy who looked to be about fifteen climbed out of the driver's seat. The girl who got out on the passenger side was probably a year or so younger. Her dark-brown hair swung about her shoulders as she jumped to the ground.

"We shouldn't be out here," she said.

"You worry too much."

"If my dad found out, he'd never let me ride to school with you again. I'd be stuck on the bus until graduation."

"Nobody's going to see us, so nobody will tell your dad."

The boy crossed in front of the vehicle and the couple started kissing, a tonsil-sucking kind of kiss that seemed years beyond the stage where these two should have been. When they came up for air, the girl broke away from the boy's embrace and took off running into the woods, thankfully in the opposite direction from where Ross and Diana were hiding and watching.

The boy pulled out a smoke, lit it, then followed the girl. Marijuana. Diana's nose puckered at the odor.

Ross leaned in close, his lips to her ear. "When I squeeze your hand, take off running toward the Jeep as fast as you can."

"What if the boy took the key with him?"

"Not likely. There's no reason to out here."

Ross waited until the two teenagers had shared a few puffs and had locked lips again before he made his move. Diana followed his lead, clearing the space between them and the Jeep in seconds. Still, by the time she'd jumped into the passenger seat, Ross had the motor sputtering to life.

"Hey, you! What the hell do you think you're doing?"

Ross smiled and waved to the frantic young man. Then he jerked the gear into reverse and gunned the engine. The tires spun in the mud, then caught and held as Ross headed the Jeep back toward the highway.

"What about them?" Diana asked, pointing to the girl and boy who were running behind the Jeep and losing ground with each stride.

"They'll walk to the road and get a ride into town. Of course, the poor girl will be riding the bus to school until she graduates."

"Good. That's where she needs to be." Diana yanked her seat belt across her stomach and buckled it. "What about us? Where are we going?"

"You tell me. This is your game."

"I haven't thought that far ahead yet."

"You're on the run from a kidnapper who wants you back so badly he spent all night in a raging storm searching for you. And you're riding with an escaped prisoner in a very distinguishable vehicle. I suggest you think of someplace fast."

Unfortunately, Diana drew a complete blank.

CONAN STOOD at the pay phone waiting for the big man to come on the line. The phone call would be short. The boss was a man of few words. He didn't want to know any details unless he specifically asked for them. And nobody ever questioned him. At least not to his face.

"Where is Diana Kincaid?"

The voice was sharp, the words clipped. Sweat broke

out on Conan's face and dampened his armpits. "I lost her."

"You lost her! Keeping her under your watch was your main responsibility, and you lost her. I thought you were capable of handling this job. I guess I was wrong."

"It wasn't my fault, sir."

"It was your job."

"I can have her back in my hands again before the sun goes down."

"Does that mean you know where she is?"

"No, but she was with some cowboy the last I saw of her. They can't have gone far."

"Some cowboy. You let *one* jerk cowboy keep you from doing the most important job you've ever been given."

"He attacked me from behind. There was nothing I could do."

"Find her. Take her home and make very sure that this kidnapping can never be traced to me."

"But I thought—"

"You do not get paid to think. You get paid to follow orders, and you haven't done a very good job of that. If you had, we'd be able to return her baby and let this all die down. Now that's impossible."

"But she can identify me. The plan was for her to—"

"The plan *is* whatever I say it is. Do you understand?"

"Yes, sir. I'll take care of everything, sir."

"Good. Take whoever you need to get the job done. And make it quick. This operation has already blown out of control."

"Consider it done."

"I hope so. For my sake. And for yours."

Conan stood in the mist, the conversation he'd just had with the boss echoing through his mind. If he followed orders, the big man himself would come out of all this smelling like a rose but Diana could identify him and he'd wind up in jail for the rest of his natural life. Governor Kincaid would see to that and the boss would do nothing to stop it from happening. He didn't tolerate mistakes.

So Conan would have to take this into his own hands. Diana Kincaid would be going back to her father. Soon. But she'd be going home in a body bag.

## Chapter Eight

"We're actually out of the woods," Diana commented when her heart stopped racing enough she could notice details.

"As long as you're talking literally."

"I am. I see a stretch of open road in front of me. That seems as good as a miracle right now."

The Jeep bounced along the two-lane highway, jostling her painful muscles, but still it was a hundred times better than walking. There were no gnats courting her eyelashes and no mosquitoes buzzing about her ears. Even better, there were no snakes slithering underfoot.

She stretched and noticed the red cellular phone resting on the seat between them. Contact with the outside world. It seemed strange that it could be so close after days without it.

She ran her fingers across the hard plastic of the phone, then picked it up, hating the fact that after what she'd learned earlier this morning, she felt more anxiety than relief over the prospect of talking to her dad.

He'd be thankful she was safe, but he would expect her to return home immediately. And if he found out she'd had her baby and that Alexandra was missing, he'd never stay out of this. This would become his fight.

But Diana didn't want a fight, didn't want to champion a cause or be part of a conflict bigger than herself. She wanted Alexandra back in her arms. Nevertheless, she had to let him and her mother know that she was safe.

Before she could finish dialing the number, Ross reached over and lay his hand on top of hers. "I've been thinking about what you said about not going to your family or to the authorities."

"It's what I have to do."

"That's not the way you felt before this morning. What happened to change your mind?"

She hesitated. There had been no reason to tell Ross who she was in the beginning and every reason not to. If she told him the truth now, he'd be angry with her for lying to him, might even walk out on their bargain. If he found out she was the governor's daughter, he'd probably run anyway. He didn't need any more notoriety at this point.

Ross's gaze left the road long enough to shoot a dubious look her way. "Something must've happened. What was it?"

She twisted in her seat so that she could watch his expression. "The man who found me this morning..." She hesitated as she sought the right words.

"My question was simple, Diana. All I expect is a simple answer."

"I'm sorry, Ross, but my life is complex, apparently more so than even I realized. Conan indicated that my abduction wasn't for a ransom as I had assumed."

"So what was it, a car-jacking gone bad?"

"No. It appears it was an act of revenge against my father."

"What do they have against him?"

"I don't know. All Conan said was that I should be

able to figure that out for myself unless I'd been living in a bubble for the last few weeks.''

"You definitely don't seem the type to live in a bubble. So what's the deal? Has your dad crossed a friend, had a falling out, snuck around with someone's wife? Who would want to get back at him?"

"I can't be sure."

"You can do better than that. Think about it. Every man has enemies."

His voice took on a sharp edge and she wondered if Ross was talking about her father still, or if he was referring to himself. Had the rancher Ross was accused of killing been his enemy? Was he guilty? Apprehension dipped inside her, like that first bite of ice cream that sent needles of cold through your system.

She pushed her doubts aside. Who was she to judge Ross's past? The important thing now was that he was exactly the kind of man she needed, and he was willing to help her in exchange for money or a lawyer to plead his case, as long as she didn't do something to make him change his mind.

"Tell me about your father," Ross insisted. "What does he do for a living? What makes him tick? What turns him on or off?"

She pressed the palms of her hands against each other. They were clammy to her touch. Her father was a lot of things; mainly he was governor of Texas and she had to find a way to tell Ross that without having him blow a gasket. She was sure he was not a man who appreciated being lied to.

Ross peered into the rearview mirror for a few seconds, then slammed his foot on the brake. Swerving, he did a U-turn and pulled off the two-lane highway, turning into a dirt road that led back into the thicket of pines and underbrush exactly like the spot they'd just left.

Panic knocked into her stomach with a dull thud. "What are you doing? We have to keep going."

"I'm making sure that truck that's been riding my tail isn't following us."

She steadied her breath and strained to see the truck pass, then fade into a smudge of blue against the highway. The man hadn't even slowed as he'd sailed past them. For once, their luck had held.

Ross steered off the dirt road and into a clump of trees, choosing a spot that let them see the highway, but made it very unlikely a passing car would notice the brown Jeep. He lowered the window, and the dust he'd sent flying drifted into the car and filled her nostrils. She covered her nose with her hand and stifled a cough.

"The truck is long gone," she said, her nerves skidding too close to the edge to feign patience. "We don't have time to sit around here chatting. As soon as those kids get to a cop, we'll have everybody in the area looking for us."

"Exactly, and that's why this may be where I get off."

"Are you turning chicken on me, Ross Taylor?"

"Call it what you want, but unless you quit talking in circles and start shooting from the hip, you can count me out."

"I don't know what you mean. I was trying to answer your questions."

"Yeah, well, talking in circles may be fine in the group you travel in, sweetie, but I'm just a plain old cowboy. I don't dance anything fancier than a two-step, I don't eat quiche, and I don't speak any language but Texan. If you want my help, you level with me."

She sighed and rubbed her fingers along the taut muscles at the back of her neck.

"The truth, plain and simple, or I'm out of here." His face took on the hard lines of a man who meant business.

"Okay, Ross. You want the truth. Here it is, at least as much as I know of it. I'm Diana Kincaid. My dad is Governor Thomas Kincaid."

A low whistle escaped his mouth. "And exactly when were you planning to drop that little bombshell on me?"

"Today."

"That's mighty thoughtful of you."

"All right, I admit I should have told you from the first, but I didn't trust you then. You showed up in handcuffs and you admitted you were wanted for murder. I had no reason to think you wouldn't hold me for ransom the same way those monsters were if you knew my dad was in a position of power."

"Or if I'd known he was one of the wealthiest men in Texas. Which explains why you had no qualms about offering me large sums of money." He stretched his right arm along the back of the seat. "Your family's powerful and rich, so why are you determined to go this alone? And no double-talk this time. I'm either in all the way or I'm out."

He was right. She couldn't half trust him and expect him to be able to help her. It was a full partnership or nothing. "Originally I thought I'd been kidnapped for ransom," she explained. "If that was the case, my getting free would put an end to it. I'd be safe and the cops would be the best people to track down my missing daughter."

"Ransom or revenge, I think you should go to the

cops and to your dad. They're a lot more qualified to handle this than we are. Besides, they have guns.''

"No. I want to leave my dad out of this. If I go public with the details, I'll give the men responsible for the baby-napping exactly what they're looking for. Notoriety. It will become a war between them and my dad and Alexandra will be the pawn. I refuse to let that happen. I just want to find her and get her back before she ends up…''

The sentence faded to silence. She absolutely couldn't say the word that logically followed. Couldn't even think it. Alexandra was alive. She felt it deep inside her, a silken cord that kept her heart from exploding into a million jagged pieces.

Ross stared past her, his brows furrowed into thin lines. "What makes you think your dad hasn't already gone to the authorities? You told Conan this morning that you were sure the cops were already searching for you.''

"That was just a ploy to try to get him to let me go free. But I know my father well. While I can't be sure he hasn't turned this over to the police, I do know he doesn't trust the cops. He complains that half of them are bought and paid for by the mob. Besides, he likes to be the man in control. My guess is that he'll be looking for me, but he'll be doing it his way, using men he trusts.''

"Like father, like daughter. There must have been some serious head-butting in your family.''

"How did you guess?''

"If your father's way works, I say go with it. He's got the funds to hire a whole crew of private detectives, bodyguards, whoever he wants. Let him run the show.''

A sharp burst of pain attacked Diana's right temple.

Using the tips of her three middle fingers, she tried to massage it away. "I'd go to the cops, my father or the devil himself if I thought it would help, but I truly believe I have a better chance of getting Alexandra back if I can do this quietly. I don't want a battle of wills, Dad against some unknown force. I just want my daughter back. But there's more."

"I was afraid there might be."

"Conan said my daughter was sold on the black market." Her voice grew shaky as the thought tore into her attempt to stay in control. "Sold—as if she were a sack of flour. What kind of people would do such a thing?"

He touched a hand to her shoulder. She looked up and saw that his face had drawn into a deep scowl and his eyes had darkened to pools of ebony. At that moment, she could well believe him capable of killing a man, and the realization made her blood run cold. She pulled away from his touch.

"I'll tell you what kind of people do those things. Men with no conscience. Men like J. B. Crowe."

She'd heard of Crowe, even met him a time or two. He looked like every other businessman she ran into at charity functions in Dallas, but she knew his reputation as well. He was the alleged head of the Texas mafia and the only man she'd ever felt her dad truly hated. But still the idea of his being behind the events of the last week seemed preposterous.

"Surely you don't think this is the work of the mob."

"It has their signature all over it. Besides, you may have been living in a bubble the last few weeks, Diana, but I haven't. Your father has been on the news every night and catching front-page headlines. He's declared war on organized crime in Texas in general and J. B. Crowe in particular."

"But the mob deals with drugs and big-time racketeering—not with kidnapping and stealing babies."

"They deal in whatever J. B. Crowe says they deal in." Ross said the man's name as if it were a curse.

"Do you know him personally?" she asked, her mind still dealing with the possibility that the mob had stolen her child.

"I know him. Too well."

"But not as a friend, I take it."

"Definitely not as a friend."

Ross sat next to her, but she felt as if he were a million miles away. He'd slid inside himself, probably fighting more of his own demons.

She took a deep breath and faced him. "I want Alexandra back. If that means going up against the mob, so be it."

"Then count me in." He turned the key in the ignition and brought the Jeep to life. "Call your family. Tell them you're safe, but if they haven't heard from the kidnappers that you've given birth, don't tell them. If we're going to do this, we don't want anyone to know where we are or what we're up to."

He yanked the Jeep into gear and headed back to the highway as she dialed the number. Her dad answered on the first ring, but she barely recognized his voice. It was thick and husky with worry.

"Dad, it's me."

"Diana." His voice cracked on her name and she could tell he was fighting back tears. "Are you all right?"

"I'm fine, Dad." She kept her voice light, reassuring. "Couldn't be better."

"But we got a call that you'd been kidnapped. I have a secret task force searching everywhere for you."

Then he didn't know about the baby. Didn't know for sure that she'd actually been kidnapped. Her mind whirled and her heart pounded as she settled on a story that just might work. "I can't imagine why people play those sick pranks," she said, trying desperately to keep her voice level. "Too bad they can't get a life."

"Are you saying you weren't kidnapped?"

"Dad, if I were kidnapped, I'd be screaming for help."

"But the caller—"

"Was another kook. Do you think they have these sick minds in every state or does Texas have a monopoly on them?"

"I'm sure they're everywhere."

She could tell from his voice that he wasn't totally convinced she was telling the truth. She'd have to think of something to seal the lie. "I hope you didn't shell out money thinking you were saving me."

"No, there was no ransom request. That was what had us so confused."

"See. Just a fruitcake with a phone. Maybe there should be a background check for buying a phone the same way there is for buying a gun."

"But if you weren't kidnapped, where have you been? Your mother has been trying to reach you for days."

"I needed to get away for a while, relax a little before the baby's born. You know how I hate waiting for anything." The words were like poison as they slid across her lips. She'd never been able to get a lie past her dad, and she knew she wasn't doing it very convincingly now. But if she told him the truth, the search for Alexandra would be out of her hands. And right now finding Alexandra took precedence over everything. She longed to question him about his recent dealings with Crowe, but she didn't dare. "I'm with a friend, Dad, and I'm fine."

"I called all your friends. No one had heard from you."

"You don't know this friend. He was one of Alex's classmates in med school. I ran into him in town and he invited me up to his lake house for a few days and I decided at the spur of the moment to take him up on it."

"You could have at least called, set your mother's mind at ease."

"I'm sorry, Dad. I forget how she worries since I've become pregnant. And I had no idea you'd gotten a crank call saying I was in danger. Tell mother that for me."

"You can tell her yourself. She's napping, but I'll wake her."

Holding the phone away from her mouth, Diana took in a huge gulp of air before going on. "No, don't bother Mother if she's resting. I'll call her when I get home."

"And when will that be?"

"I'm not sure." Her answer was met with silence. She waited, knowing her father would not let it go at that.

"Diana, are you sure you're all right?"

"Absolutely."

"Tell me where you are. I'll call my office in Dallas and have them send a driver for you."

"That's not necessary. I have to go now, but I'll call you later. And don't worry. I'm fine." She hung up the phone before he had a chance to throw a new argument at her.

"Did your dad buy *that* story?"

Ross's voice startled her. She'd been so lost in the lie she'd concocted, she'd forgotten for a minute that he was beside her. "I think he believed me, but he's not happy with me. He wants me to go home."

"That makes two of us."

"Sorry, but my mind's made up. I'm going after Alexandra, even if I have to do it by myself. But I'd rather do it with your help."

Without thinking she reached across the seat and lay her hand on his arm. The intimacy of the touch hit her the second her fingers touched his flesh. She jerked her hand away.

His gaze captured hers. "I don't bite, you know."

"I know."

"Good, because it's going to be hard to work together if you're afraid of me."

"I'm not afraid."

"In that case, I'm all yours."

She doubted that, but she'd take what help he gave all the same. But help was all she could take from him. She couldn't taint her memories of Alex with desire for a man she barely knew.

"Any ideas as to where we should start?" Ross asked.

"No. I've racked my brain ever since we climbed into the Jeep about where to get information about a black-market baby ring. I've come up with nothing."

He nudged his hat back a little farther on his head. "I have a couple of friends who might be able to help us."

She handed him the phone. "Do you know their numbers?"

"Yeah, but first things first. I need to ditch this Jeep.

We could both use some food. And a hot shower would make my day.''

"We have no money, and the only way I can get any is to go back to my house and get some credit cards or at least some identification. That would mean driving to Dallas in this stolen Jeep.''

"I have another idea. A way to get money, food, rest and maybe even a vehicle.''

"I'm not up for robbing a bank.''

"There goes my first plan.''

Diana caught hold of the armrest as Ross swerved the Jeep off of the highway and down a blacktop road. She wasn't sure where they were going, but for the first time since the kidnapping, she felt as if she were tackling life instead of waiting for it to stamp her into the ground. She liked the feeling.

DIANA RELAXED a little as Ross took to the back roads, driving as fast as was safe what with school buses and an occasional farm tractor to deal with. The day was sunny and bright, the temperature already climbing high enough that the wind through the open window was warm on her face.

She stared out at the passing scenery as they left the piney woods and rolled through farm and cattle land. A thousand shades of green met her gaze, grass, plants and tree leaves all bursting into new life. A patch of yellow wildflowers danced in one of the pastures and a young calf sucked at its mother's teat beneath a sweet gum tree.

Spring. April.

She'd looked forward to spring for almost nine months, never imagining it would bring such terror. It was supposed to be a time of joy. The baby she and

Alex had tried to have when he was alive would finally be born. The grief over his death had been softened by the reality of having his child growing inside her.

Ross slowed as they came to a dirt road, the same way he'd done with the two others they'd crossed in the last five minutes. This time he turned east, directly into the glare of the sun. Greers Road, according to the sign that had been decorated with bullet holes. She readjusted her visor with little success. "Do you know where we're going?"

"Not exactly."

"What are you looking for?"

"My dad had a friend who used to live in this area—Jake Cousins. Hopefully, he's still around. If he is, we can stop over long enough to get cleaned up and regroup."

The possibility of food and a shower heightened her senses. "When was the last time you talked to him?"

"Eighteen months ago—when my dad died. But the only time we came out to visit was back when I was in high school. Our football team went to state, and my dad and I stopped off and spent a night with Jake after the game. I don't remember much about him or his ranch. I was too busy feeling bad about our losing the game. I was sure it was all because of my one dropped pass."

"Did the others blame you?"

"Hardly. We lost by twenty-four points, but I was young."

She tried to picture the man beside her as a high school student. The image didn't jell. She could only imagine him as he was now, tough-edged, his chin whiskered, tall and muscular, a man's man.

"I think Greers is the right road, though," Ross said. "I have a good memory for names."

"Do you think you'll recognize his house?"

"Probably not, so look for a gate with a sign that says Copper Hill."

"Are you sure we can trust this man?"

He stretched the muscles in his neck, leaning his head back and then pulling it forward a couple of times. "Jake will help if he can. My dad saved his life back in Vietnam, but I don't want to cause him any trouble. I think it's best if we don't mention who you are, just that you're a friend of mine and that you've agreed to help me hire a lawyer and clear up the mess I got in back in Halpern."

"Maybe you shouldn't even tell him that you're wanted for murder."

"I won't have to. Your dad may have kept your disappearance quiet, but I'm a danger to the innocent public. I'm sure everyone in East Texas has been warned to be on the lookout for me. By now they've probably figured out that I have a woman with me and that we're the ones who stole the Jeep from the teenagers. They'll be looking for a couple."

A couple—she and Ross. The connotation wasn't accurate, yet it fit in some inexplicable way. Not the way she and Alex had been a couple, but bound all the same, by coincidence and need and trust. If she found Alexandra, she'd owe him a lot, far more than she'd ever be able to pay him.

"THIS IS IT," Ross announced as he pulled up to a closed gate. The sign that dangled from the top rail by one lone piece of twisted wire assured him that he had indeed found Copper Hill. He jumped out of the Jeep and unlatched the gate, watching and listening to it squeak as it swung open.

Once through the gate, he climbed back out and closed it behind them. The best two ways to keep your welcome, his dad used to say. Don't overstay your visit and close the gate behind you.

Dust rose in thick clouds as they headed toward a small house with a large porch. The paint was faded and peeling, and one of the shutters was missing. A row of leaning bricks marked what used to be a flower bed next to the steps, but it was overgrown with grass and weeds.

"I don't think anyone lives—"

Before Diana could finish her sentence, a man stepped out the front door, letting the screen door bang shut behind him. If the man was Jake Cousins he'd changed a lot in the eighteen years since Ross had last seen him. His hair had thinned considerably and turned gray. His shoulders were stooped, his face dry and weathered.

Ross waved as he parked the Jeep beneath the shade of a persimmon tree.

The man stepped to the edge of the porch. "You folks lost?"

"I don't know," Ross said, stepping out of the Jeep. "Are you Jake Cousins?"

"I am unless my mom took the wrong brat home from the hospital and raised me."

"Then we're at the right place."

Jake leaned over the edge of the porch and spit a stream of tobacco into the weeds. "In that case, what can I do for you?"

"I'm Melvin Taylor's son."

Jake squinted and leaned against a support post. "Melvin's boy, are you?"

"I am."

He slid his hands into the deep pockets of his overalls. "You do favor Melvin a little, but you look a hell of a lot better. Better than that police drawing they showed of you on TV, too."

"So you've heard?"

"Yep. We don't get a lot of excitement in this part of the world. An escaped convict's almost as good as a celebrity."

Ross winced. "I figured as much."

"Half of the cops in East Texas are probably out looking for you right now. Of course, if they're using that drawing they showed on the TV to identify you, they might not know you if you walked up and bit them on the behind."

"What else did they say about me?"

"That you killed a rancher over in Halpern."

"I didn't."

"I didn't think so, not unless you had a damn good reason for doing it. Melvin raised you better than that." He nodded toward Diana. "Is that your wife?"

"No, this is Diana. She's just a friend." Diana rounded the Jeep and Ross put a hand to the small of her back. "We don't want to cause any problems for you but I was hoping we could trouble you for a meal."

Jake's gaze settled first on Diana and then swung back to Ross. "I can rustle you up some food. You can use a shower, too. You look like you've been wrestling with pigs in a mud hole."

"We've been in the woods for a couple of days. I hate to come to you, Jake, but I didn't know where else to turn. Still, if you'd rather we keep driving, just say the word."

"I'd have a hard time living with myself if I turned Melvin's son down for a favor. That's not a good place to leave that Jeep, though. Park it in the barn back behind the house. There's plenty of room in there."

"I appreciate that."

"Diana, why don't you come inside with me? A woman in the family way shouldn't be standing out in sun this bright."

She ran her hands down the front of the maternity shirt, flattening the gathered fabric against her stomach. "I'm not pregnant," she said.

Ross watched her as she walked up the steps. Battered and bruised, muddy and disheveled, worn from giving birth and then going on the run, she still had a way about her. It was understated, like a whisper, but you could see it in the way she walked, the way she held her head.

Feminine. Sensual. Classy. She was way out of his league, and he needed to remember that. As soon as this was over, she'd go back to her life and leave him to his.

The life he'd made such a mess of. Fortunately, his dad wasn't here to see him now. But, he felt his dad's presence stronger than ever. And the memories never came without the familiar regret and the anger.

He felt it tightening inside him, building up until he wanted to beat his fists into something hard, ached to lash out at something. Specifically at J. B. Crowe. Only he couldn't let his fight get in the way of Diana's quest.

She wanted her baby. Ross wanted satisfaction, and that would only come if J. B. Crowe himself landed behind bars for the rest of his natural life.

and save Alexandra. The local cops had always been powerless against the mob, and there was no reason to expect things would be different this time.

Her father wasn't powerless, but if she went to him, the hate between the two men would burgeon and her chances of getting her daughter back alive would diminish proportionately.

She closed her eyes against the sting of tears that burned at the back of her eyelids, trying desperately to keep them in check. Taking the soapy cloth in hand, she rubbed briskly, easing up when she came to her breasts.

Mounds of flesh, mammary glands that should have been heavy with milk, nourishment for Alexandra. Evidently, the doc had thought of that, too. One of the drugs he'd shot into her system must have been to dry up her milk, another part of motherhood that had been stolen from her. She touched the tips of her nipples and a wave of heartbreak washed across her.

She gave up fighting the tears. Her hormones were out of sync and her heart was breaking, and all she could do was stand there and face the images that battered her mind.

Was another woman rocking Alexandra to sleep and singing her lullabies? Was another woman sharing the first wonderful days of life, bonding with her baby, the one she'd carried inside her for months and dreamed about for years before that? Her baby, but Diana's arms were empty and her heart felt as if someone had lanced it and bled it dry. But she prayed that another woman was keeping her safe and loved until Diana could find her and take her home.

A light tap sounded at the door, and she jumped as if it had been a gun blast.

"Are you all right in there?"

She reached up and turned off the faucets. "I'm fine." She'd tried to sound normal, but she knew Ross would hear the hoarseness in her voice and know she was crying. Nothing got past him. Another reason she'd wanted him on her side. "I'm getting out now."

"Take as long as you need. I was just checking to make sure you hadn't collapsed in there. You've got to be running on empty."

Her wet feet slapped against the bare tiles as she stepped from the shower and grabbed one of the towels Jake had put out for them. Not luxuriously fluffy like the ones in her own bath, but functional, the way Jake Cousins lived. A simple man with simple values, and she was very lucky that those values included helping the son of a friend.

Running the towel down her bare legs to catch the last drops of moisture, she noticed that she could bend a little easier than she had yesterday. In spite of tramping through the woods only a few days after giving birth, her body was recuperating.

She draped the towel over the doorknob and slipped her arms through the blue cotton shirt Jake had given her to wear while her own mud-splattered clothes churned in the washing machine. Jake's shirt was sizes too big, but it smelled of detergent and sunshine and it was clean. She rolled up the sleeves a few notches so that her hands could peek out. The tail of the shirt hit her knee-high, but she still felt a little indecent knowing she'd have nothing on beneath the soft cotton but her panties.

Grabbing a dry towel, this one only slightly more thirsty than the first, she twisted it over her wet hair and opened the bathroom door. Ross was standing in the hall when she came out, waiting to make sure she was all right and not dissolving into a sobbing basket case.

"The shower's all yours," she said, "though I'm afraid I may have hogged more than my share of the hot water."

"I'd say you earned the privilege." He wiped his thumb beneath her right eye. "You've been crying."

"I guess I'm not as strong as I like to think."

"Nothing hurts, does it? I mean, I know you're sore, but do you think there are physical—"

"I'm healing fine. I just want to get started. No, I want to get *finished*. I want my daughter."

"Diana."

He paused and she lifted her gaze to lock with his. His eyes seemed darker in the dim light of the hall, more intense. Troubled. "You found out something while I was showering, didn't you? What is it, Ross? Is it about Alexandra?"

"No. It's about your father."

She didn't have to ask if it was bad news. His tone said it all. "What about my dad?"

"Someone planted a bomb in his office. Fortunately it didn't detonate."

A bomb. Power to blow a man to bits. She felt the pressure building inside her, stealing her breath and making her queasy. "How did you find out?"

"It was on the noon news."

"Do they know who did it?"

"Nothing beyond speculation and no one's claimed credit for the attempt."

"This may not be connected to my kidnapping at all, Ross. There have been bomb threats before. Once it was just a disgruntled maintenance man at the capitol."

Ross looked down at her, the lines around his eyes

and mouth falling into deep grooves. "This wasn't an idle threat, Diana. If the bomb had worked properly, you father might be dead."

He took her hands in his. "I don't want to upset you any more than you already are, Diana, but this may be developing into an all-out war. And I'm not an army. I'm only one man, unarmed, running from the law."

The frustration of the situation ground inside her. "Don't tell me you want to back out again?"

"Not for myself, but there's no way I can protect you against everything these people can hurl your way."

"So are you saying you think I should just surrender and let the dirty cowards win? Because if you are, you don't know me at all, Ross Taylor."

"All I'm saying is that you should go home and let your father's men protect you."

"They didn't do that good a job of protecting him. Besides, protecting me wasn't the deal we made." She pushed inside his space, face-to-face, her body ravaged by a frigid chill that reached deep inside her. "*I'm* going to find my baby."

"And how is it you plan to go about that? If it is Crowe you're up against, he's dodged every law enforcement agency in Texas for years."

"I don't know, but I will." She was shaking now, from the chill and the determination. "I just will."

He took her into his arms and held her. Her first impulse was to pull away, but once she felt his strength and warmth wrap around her, she leaned into him. Ross rested his chin on the top of her head and held her until she'd quit trembling. But even after he'd released her with his arms, his gaze still held her, a penetrating stare that said they'd crossed one more line in their uneasy alliance.

"You just don't give up do you?" he said.

"Only when I have to."

"Then you leave me no choice. I'll stand beside you." He took her hand and led her to a bedroom just off the narrow hallway. "We can't stay here long, so you need to rest while you can."

"Is Jake upset that we're here?"

"No, but he's a little nervous. I don't blame him for that. Still, he insists we eat and get some rest before we start out again."

"Then he believes you're innocent?"

"So he says, but he thinks I should give myself up. And he wanted to know who you are."

"You didn't tell him?"

"I said you were my woman." He walked over and pulled down the quilt. "This is our room, so don't worry about messing up the covers."

"*Our* room?"

"Well, if you're my woman I could hardly ask for two beds."

"No, of course not. We're adults. We can handle lying on the same bed without making it into something sexual."

He stared at her, letting his gaze linger on the swell of her breasts before it moved to her bare legs. "I'm a red-blooded man, Diana. Not a eunuch."

She blushed at the desire that colored his words, then reddened even more at the rush of heat that swept through her body. It seemed wrong to feel any kind of attraction at a time like this, yet she couldn't deny it. Couldn't deny that she'd liked being in Ross's arms a minute ago. But then, when a woman had been without a man as long as she had, it shouldn't surprise her that someone as sexy as Ross Taylor would affect her on some primitive level.

Guilt surfaced again, the sense that she was betraying Alex. Rationally she knew that she couldn't betray a dead man, but still the feeling persisted.

The best move would be to go to the kitchen and help Jake with the cooking, but one look at the clean white sheets, and she dropped to the side of the bed. "I think I will rest for a minute. If I happen to fall asleep, wake me in time to eat. Whatever Jake's cooking smells divine."

"I'll wake you." He pulled the quilt over her and tucked it under her chin.

She turned away.

"You don't need to add me to your worry list, Diana. I may be a little rough around the edges, a tad backward in the manners department, but I've never forced myself on a woman. I don't plan to start now. I won't touch you unless it's what you want, but neither will I pretend that being with you doesn't affect me."

With that he turned and disappeared through the bedroom door. His comment didn't relieve her worries in the least. Whether she should or not, she had liked his touch. Liked it very, very much.

ROSS SHED HIS SHIRT, dropped his pants and shorts and deposited them outside the bathroom door just as Jake was coming down the hall to collect them for the washing machine. He waved, then closed the door and stepped into the tile stall. He'd planned on a hot shower, been craving one ever since he left that two-bit roach-infested jail, but holding Diana in his arms had changed all of that. Now he needed the water icy cold.

He had no business getting turned on by a woman

like Diana Kincaid. He had no business getting hot and bothered by anyone while his life was in such a mess. Wanted for murder with no defense except that he'd gotten hit over the head and knocked out cold. Even the fancy lawyer Diana had promised him wouldn't get too far with that story. Not that he'd hold her to the bargain they'd made this morning. He wasn't helping her for what he could get in return.

He wasn't helping her for some noble reason like he just wanted to see justice done, either. He'd given up on that a year ago, right before he'd left Texas. He was helping her because there was no way he could look into those haunted emerald eyes and say no.

And because this might finally be his chance to nail J. B. Crowe to the wall. For a while getting the man had been an obsession, the fuel that had kept Ross going day after day with nothing to show for his actions except defeat. Crowe had bested him at every turn, pulled the rug right out from under his feet along with his career as a detective on the Dallas Police Force. Finally, Ross had walked away from the hate and the vengeance, knowing if he didn't it would destroy him completely.

Only the fury had returned now, and this time he knew he'd never walk away until Crowe was in prison or until Ross lay in a wood coffin six feet under the ground. But, whatever he did, he had to keep Diana Kincaid safe, had to succeed where he'd failed so miserably before.

He finished showering, dried off and wrapped a towel around his waist while he shaved. The razor dragged across the two-day-old mat of facial hair, and it took twice as long as usual to get rid of the whiskers.

He stared into the mirror when he was finished. Clean shaven and without his jeans and boots, he was just like any other man. It wasn't as if the label Poor Jerk was tattooed on his forehead or emblazoned on his chest. He could pass for one of the rich, socially acceptable guys who attended soirees at the governor's mansion. Hell, he was probably better-looking and smarter than a lot of them.

He shook his head and looked away from the image that mocked him. "You're just an out-of-work cowboy these days, Ross Taylor. Nothing more. Except now you can add escaped prisoner to your résumé."

"Ross. Please. Help me!"

The scream sliced into his thoughts and he yanked open the bathroom door, his heart slamming against his chest. The towel began to slide down around his hips, and he yanked it up again, gripping it with his right fist as he raced down the hall and pushed through the bedroom door.

His adrenaline slowed, then settled like hot mush in his stomach. It was Diana's scream, all right, but she was in bed alone, tossing and grappling with the quilt.

"Ross. He's coming. Don't leave me."

His heart twisted into a thousand jagged shreds. She was reliving the nightmare, but this time it wasn't her dead husband she was calling for. He stepped to the bed and sat on the edge, taking her hand in his.

"It's okay, Diana. I'm here. You're safe."

She quieted, though she didn't open her eyes. He stayed with her, balanced on the edge of the thin mattress, watching the accelerated rise and fall of her chest as she fell back into a restless sleep. The towel she'd had around her head had fallen loose, and the damp strands curled around her cheeks and over her forehead.

Asleep, she looked girlish, innocent. Beautiful. He stared a minute longer, his thoughts going crazy, imagining what it would be like to make love to a woman like Diana. No, not *like* Diana. He wondered what it would be like to make love with Diana. Would she want to control the lovemaking the way she did the search for her child or would she purr contentedly while he roamed her body with his eager hands? Would she cry out with delight when she climaxed, or would she slide quietly into the orgasm?

He closed his eyes, his body alive and aching to discover the answers to the questions his mind asked. But he was only tormenting himself, wondering about things he'd never know, reeling from desire and needs that would never be satisfied—at least not by the woman who spawned them.

Forcing his body to follow sensible commands, he rose from the bed and walked to the door. Jake would have the food ready soon, but before they ate, he needed to make a phone call to his old buddy from his days on the Dallas Police Force. Dylan Garrett was one of the few men who had ever fully infiltrated the Mafia and walked away. If anyone could supply him with information about the baby-smuggling ring, it would be Dylan.

Or Zach Logan, and he hated the idea of begging for information from the man who'd fired him from a job that had become his life. Strange how the past had blown up in his face again. And all because he'd returned to Texas and stumbled upon a woman held captive in the woods.

THE TELEPHONE RANG, stopping Dylan Garrett just as he was about to pull the office door shut behind him. Any other morning, he'd have answered without even thinking, but today was different. Things were heating up in the battle between Thomas Kincaid and J. B. Crowe and his old boss Zach Logan had pleaded with him to come back to Dallas one more time. They needed the knowledge he'd acquired during his stint as an undercover agent deep inside the Crowe compound.

Still, the call could be important. He strode to the phone and checked the caller ID. Out of area. That was a big help. He let it ring one more time and then yanked it up.

"Finders Keepers. Dylan Garrett speaking."

"So you really did leave the big-city detective life to move back to the ranch?"

"To the ranch and Finders Keepers, the best private detective agency in all of Texas." He glanced at his watch. Zach Logan didn't like to be kept waiting. "Who is this?"

"Ross Taylor."

He muttered a word his mother would have washed his mouth out with soap for saying and perched on the edge of his desk. "Where the hell are you and how did you wind up in that mess in Halpern?"

"Just lucky, I guess. Anyway, that's not what I'm calling about."

"You're wanted for murder. You escaped from the sheriff while he was transporting you to another jail, and now you've stolen a Jeep from a couple of high school kids. But that's not what you're calling about. You haven't changed a bit."

"I'm older. Uglier."

"But hopefully not more stupid. So what's the story?"

"There's this woman—"

Dylan groaned. "The downfall of man. I should have

guessed. I suppose this is the woman you were with when you stole the Jeep."

"Boy, news does travel fast."

"So, hit the high points. Who is she and what's her problem?"

"Her name's not important, but she's searching for a missing baby, one born only a few days ago."

"Is the baby hers?"

"Yeah. Do you know if there's a baby-smuggling ring operating in Texas?"

"As a matter of fact, it appears that there is, mostly down in the southwest part of the state, but there are rumors of activities in the area between Dallas and San Antonio as well."

"Is Crowe behind the ring?"

"Not that anyone can prove, but if it's illegal and makes money, he's usually either running the whole deal or at least getting a cut. Actually, Finders Keepers has been looking into it—in regard to a missing child."

"Do you have anything concrete?"

"Nothing hard and fast, but we've picked up a few soft leads."

"Can you give me what you have?"

"I've got to run, but Lily can fill you in. You do remember my sister, don't you?"

"Naturally. She's the pretty one of the family. Smart, too, if I remember correctly. Is she running the P.I. business with you?"

"Yeah, and she's damn good at it. If you hold on, I'll call her and she can give you any pertinent details."

"Thanks."

"Better yet, Ross, why don't you send the woman to us? I'll get Lily or one of my associates to handle her case and you can turn yourself in. If you don't, you're biting off a chunk of trouble you may not be able to swallow."

"Aren't you going to ask me if I'm guilty?"

Dylan pulled up a memory or two. He and Ross working the streets of Dallas before he'd gone undercover. Ross had been the best partner a cop ever had and Dylan had seen him put his life on the line more than once protecting him and the citizens of Dallas. He'd been one hell of a cop, right until the deal with Crowe had blown up in his face and he'd lost all perspective.

"I don't need to ask if you're guilty, Ross. If you pulled a gun, you had reason. If you pulled the trigger, it was to save a life."

"Thanks, buddy."

"Thanks not necessary. Just take my advice and turn yourself in."

"Yeah, soon. One other question. Do you know anything more than what was released to the media about the bomb in the governor's office?"

Dylan hesitated. He was on Zach's payroll again and he wasn't at liberty to say anything of what they suspected, not even to Ross. Secrets and lying to his friends. That was what he'd hated most about working undercover. "I don't know any more than what was on the news," he said, not actually lying. "Don't tell me you're taking on the governor's problems, too."

"Just curious. I know Crowe's got to be agitated with Kincaid's stand on ridding the Mafia from the state of Texas."

Dylan's hand tightened on the receiver. "Let the past go, Ross. It's cost you too much already."

"Nice talking to you, Dylan."

"I hope you listened to me."

"I always listen. Now, how about getting Lily for me."

Dylan walked away from the phone. Ross Taylor was in deep trouble. A woman could do that to you, especially if you fell for the wrong one.

No one knew that better than Dylan.

JAKE STUCK HIS HEAD into the den where Ross was mulling over the information he'd gotten from Lily. "The food's about ready. Hope you're hungry."

"Hungry enough I could eat a cow cooked over a branding iron."

"If I'd known that I wouldn't have bothered cooking the meat."

Ross padded across the kitchen to check out the menu. There were chunks of potatoes, smothered in onions, frying in a cast-iron skillet on the back of the range. A pan of milk gravy simmered on the front burner and a trio of steaks sizzled under the broiler.

"You've gone all out. Where did you learn to cook like this?"

"Taught myself when my wife up and left me, and that's been a hundred or so years ago." He cracked an egg and let it spill into a crockery bowl. "Your clothes aren't dry yet," Jake said, reaching for the next egg, "but there's a robe hanging on a hook inside my closet. I'm not too keen on sittin' at the table with a man wearing nothing but an appetite and a towel."

"The robe it is, but first I need to ask you one more favor."

"Long as I got a biscuit, you got half. I'll do what I can, as long as it's not illegal."

"Aiding and abetting an escaped prisoner is illegal, and you've already done that."

"Well, there you go. I've already broke the only rule I live by, so you name it, and it's good as done."

ROSS EXCHANGED the towel for the robe, then stopped at the bedroom where he'd left Diana sleeping. Her eyes fluttered open and she rubbed them sleepily. He stepped closer.

"Your whiskers are gone," she said, squinting up at him. "You look different."

He ran his fingers along his smooth chin. "Different as in better, I hope."

"Very nice. The mud's gone, too."

"Goes to show that you can even clean up a cowboy if you have enough soap."

She started to sit up, but groaned instead and grabbed her back. "Too much tension," she said, forcing her lips to stretch into a smile though he could see the pain in her eyes.

"Is there something I can do to help?"

"Maybe. How are you at back rubs?"

He held out his hands. "I've never had any complaints."

"Talk's cheap. Show me." She kicked off the quilt and rolled over on her stomach, punctuating the movement with a few well-placed moans.

Ross considered the situation. His hands on Diana Kincaid. Stroking. Probing. And both of them in a near naked state.

And he'd thought running for his life had been dangerous.

# Chapter Ten

Ross stepped closer, reminding himself that being attracted to Diana Kincaid was like smelling whiskey through a jailhouse window. No matter how much it tempted you, you weren't going to be invited to indulge. He sat down beside her. "I can't believe little things like having a baby and taking a hike in the woods put you in this condition," he joked.

"My friends warned me that once I passed thirty, I'd fall apart."

"So what are you now, an old woman of thirty-one?"

"Thirty-four."

"I've still got you beat by two years."

"If I keep aging as fast as I have this week, I may catch up." She moved an inch to the left and dissolved into a new wave of groans. "I didn't wait until I was thirty to have pain, though. I became fast friends with it when I turned a motorcycle into a flying space machine during my sophomore year at Tulane University."

"A Hells Angel, huh? I bet the governor loved that."

"He threatened to disown me, but a threat to disown me was part of our standard Sunday afternoon conversations during my college years."

"The rebellious daughter. I can see it now. Diana in

body-hugging leather riding up on a Harley. Any tattoos I should check out?''

"Only if you're a doctor or if I get to know you *very* well."

He didn't dare touch that remark. "Where's it hurt the most? The lower back or in the shoulders?"

"Right here." She used her fingers to guide him to the spot. "It feels as if someone tied knots in my backbone."

He flexed his hands, then placed them on the small of her back. His fingers splayed across her hips while his thumbs rode her spine. Not surprisingly, the muscles beneath his hands were coiled like a spring that had been wound too tightly.

Hard, yet soft. A contradiction, like everything else about her. The governor's daughter, but with a mind of her own and a tattoo to prove it. Slowly and methodically, he applied pressure, and with each stroke, his body reacted in ways it was going to be difficult to hide. Sweat plastered his brow, and the area around his groin twitched and roared painfully to life.

She stretched and Jake's blue chambray shirt inched up her thighs. Nice thighs. Tanned. Shapely. He clenched his hands into fists and pulled away.

"I can't do this, Diana."

"Sure you can. You've got great hands."

His breath exploded from his lungs. "It's not the hands. It's the rest of me."

She rolled over to her side. One look, and he knew she understood exactly what he meant. There was no mistaking the bulge beneath his robe.

He wouldn't have been surprised if she'd ordered him out of the room. Instead she let her gaze linger. "I'm sorry. I guess being with a near naked woman could do strange things to a man's libido.''

"But not to yours?"

"I haven't been with a man in almost two years, Ross. All you have to do is be nice to me, treat me like a woman and I'm bound to feel something.''

"Aren't you having a little trouble with your math?''

"What do you mean?''

"Unless I failed the birds-and-bees lesson, it takes two to make a baby, and you had to have gotten pregnant about nine months ago.''

"The birds and the bees have become technologically complex. My husband and I were undergoing fertility treatments before he was killed in a boating accident. His sperm was frozen. Alexandra is his baby.''

He shuffled his bare feet against the rough wooden floor planks. "I'm sorry. When you said your husband had been dead for nearly two years, I just assumed there must be someone else between him and now. Not that it was any of my business.''

"No. There's never been anyone else, not since the day I met him.''

"Alex was a lucky man, to have a woman love him so much that she still wanted to have his baby even after he was no longer with her.''

"He's dead, Ross. How lucky can that be?'' She threw her legs over the side of the bed and stood, wincing as she straightened her back. "I think it's better if we just leave our pasts out of this. Our bargain is just about the present. You help me get Alexandra back, I furnish you with the best lawyer I can find. The less personally involved we get, the better it will be for both of us.''

"You got it. All business.'' He leaned against the

door frame, watching her finger comb the glorious masses of red curls into a semblance of order. And even while he was mouthing the words, he was struggling with the attraction for her that just kept on coming. Like a truck with no brakes heading down a steep hill.

He forced his mind back to his conversation with Dylan. "Speaking of business, I made a few phone calls while you were resting."

"Did you find out something that would help us find Alexandra?"

"Nothing concrete, but I did get some leads on a baby-selling ring that's been operating in this area and in South Texas."

"Oh, Ross, this could be exactly what we're looking for."

She latched onto the possibility eagerly, and he hated to burst her bubble. But he couldn't let her start thinking it was a sure thing either. "It's just a lead, Diana. I have names and addresses of a couple of women about fifty miles south of Dallas. One reported that she was contacted about selling her baby. The other one thinks her daughter may have gotten rid of her child illegally."

"How horrible. Babies sold like vegetables being carted to market."

"Hopefully, these women will give us something we can use. All we have to do is keep me out of the hands of the police a little while longer so that we have a chance to interview them."

"We don't have any means of transportation, Ross. If we get on the road in that Jeep, we're sure to be apprehended."

"Jake says we can take his old pickup. That gives us a little better chance of making it."

"A chance is all we need."

Ross envied her confidence. He tended to go the other way. If there was a chance something could go wrong, it usually did. "We'll have to wait until dark and take the back roads."

"And Jake is okay with our staying here until then?"

"It was his idea. He even volunteered to get rid of the Jeep for us. He has a friend who'll help him desert it somewhere where it can be found and returned to the owner." He turned at the sound of Jake's heavy footsteps in the hall.

The old rancher stopped at the door, his hands and arms draped with their clothes. "Washed and dried and good as new. Well, actually they're not all that good. With all the rips and tears, they look like you fought off a bobcat or two. But put 'em on and get downstairs before the food gets cold."

They didn't have to be told twice.

ANNE KINCAID SAT in an antique rocker in a room she'd transformed into a nursery. The governor's mansion wasn't particularly baby friendly, but she planned to change all of that. The new nursery with its border of nursery rhyme characters was the first step. Rocking back and forth, she clutched the stuffed lamb she'd bought in anticipation of her first grandchild.

She'd picked it up last week before her world had started falling apart. First the worry that Diana was in the hands of kidnappers. Now someone planting a bomb in Thomas's office. And she was certain both situations stemmed from his problems with J. B. Crowe. The conflict between the two men had always been charged with a fury that was destined to erupt one day.

And now Thomas had made it clear. He was going to smash J.B. and all he stood for into the ground and nothing would change his mind. He said it was all for the good of Texas and maybe it was, but it was also for the good of Thomas Kincaid. A score he felt he had to settle.

She'd always heard that bad things came in threes, but she prayed that wasn't the case this time. She couldn't bear for anything to happen to Thomas or to Diana. He had told her that Diana had called, assured her as best he could that their daughter was safe. But she couldn't lose the nagging doubt in the back of her mind that something was not quite as it should be. She wouldn't until she'd talked to Diana herself.

The old Diana used to go off without telling anyone where she was going or who she was going with. But she'd been young then, trying out her wings, attempting to find herself outside her father's world. Thomas had never understood that, but Anne had. She'd often wished she could do it herself. Wished she was as independent and strong-willed as Diana had become.

It wasn't that Thomas meant to take over everyone's space. It was just that he filled a room when he walked into it, commandeered attention. She'd accepted that he needed to be in control and had learned it was easier to let him give orders and spout his words of advice than it was to argue with him. Diana had never accepted that fact, probably because she was as headstrong as he was.

The phone rang, and Anne jumped at the sound. Hurrying into the kitchen, she picked up the receiver, hoping it was Diana.

"Hello." The sound of breathing was all that greeted her. Her hands grew clammy. "Who is this?"

"A friend of Diana's."

"What do you want?"

"Just give her a message for me. Tell her that her daughter is crying for her."

Anne's hands shook as the caller broke the connection. Her stomach pitched and she felt as if she might faint dead away. Taking quick breaths, she managed to pull herself to the couch.

She didn't know what was going on, but for the first time in her life, she was sure Thomas had lied to her when he'd said Diana had called and told him she was fine. And for the first time since they'd exchanged their wedding vows, she was going to go against his wishes and take matters into her own hands.

She punched in the number for the Dallas Police Force.

"ARE YOU SURE you still want to go through with this?" Ross asked as they prepared to leave for Dallas.

"Absolutely." Diana shrugged her arms into the light jacket Jake had lent her. It fell from her shoulders and seemed to swallow her, the same way the maternity clothes did now that she no longer needed them. "I don't know why I'd have changed my mind."

"Because you could be sitting in a nice, comfortable house letting the authorities do this for you."

"I have no desire to sit and wait, but I do wish we could just stop at my house and change clothes. I feel like a refugee from a war-torn third-world country."

"We could try it."

"Not a good idea. My neighbors might notice if I came waltzing in with a man wanted for murder. Besides, there's always a chance my dad would have someone watching the house to see when I return. I'm still afraid he didn't buy my story a hundred percent."

She stopped talking as Jake entered the room carrying

a bag of sandwiches and a thermos of hot coffee for the road.

He handed Ross the bag. "Do you have the map I gave you?"

"In my pocket, with all the back roads marked."

"I just hope that old truck doesn't let you down. She's not but ten years old, but she's got some hard miles on her. You have to humor her, be nice to her the way you would a woman. If you try to manhandle her, she becomes as ornery as a spinster at her sister's wedding."

"I'll stroke her until she purrs."

"You'll get more rattles than purrs, but at least no one will have called the cops and reported it as missing. As long as you don't get caught in a roadblock somewhere, you should be fine."

They stepped onto the porch. The moon had ducked behind a mass of clouds, dimming the shadows that crept along the edge of the steps. Jake ran his hands deep in his pockets. "I still think you should go to the cops, Ross. Turn yourself in. Running, the way you're doing now, makes you look guiltier 'n sin."

"I'm going to. I just have one little bit of business to take care of first."

"This doesn't have anything to do with what happened to your dad, does it?"

"Not this time."

"Good. He'd want you to go on with your life, but he wouldn't like your running from the law like this. You're sealing the case against you, and a guilty verdict can keep you in jail for the rest of your life."

"I'm innocent, Jake. It will work out."

"God go with you, boy."

The wind blew cold on Diana's neck as they walked

to the old pickup and climbed inside. Jake's fear for Ross crawled under her skin and made her afraid, too. She had just assumed that once this was over, they could hire a lawyer and he'd take care of everything. But what if she was wrong? What if running made him appear so guilty that he'd never get off?

Ross started the truck, coaxed it into reverse and backed away from the house. Once they had cleared the gate, he lowered his foot on the accelerator and the truck shimmied and rocked down the highway.

She settled into the rhythm as Ross leaned back and stretched his right arm across the back of the seat. "Nothing like a vehicle with worn shocks and a bumpy road to get the kinks out of your system," he said. "This ride should either cure your back or put you in the hospital."

"And I thought tramping through the woods was rough."

"Tramping through the woods is fun. It was having men with guns tramping behind us that put the damper on the experience."

But his attempt at keeping the moment light didn't work. Jake's words still haunted her mind. "If you want to back out of our bargain and turn yourself in, I'll understand."

"Whoa! What prompted this turnaround?"

"I'm not giving up if that's what you think and I'm not afraid for myself. But I don't want to shoulder the responsibility for having a jury find you guilty of murder."

He trailed a finger down the back of her neck. "If I decide to run out on you, I'll let you know. In the meantime, I have another idea. We have transportation to Dallas, but we'll still need money for gas and food and a place to stay while we're investigating. We need a headquarters that would supply those things and still be a place people wouldn't ordinarily look for an escaped prisoner.''

"What kind of place would that be?"

"At the home of the governor's daughter."

She threw up her hands in exasperation. "I can't take you home with me. I've told you already that my dad may have someone watching the place."

"So let them watch. We'll walk right in, laughing and talking like old friends."

"What about the cops who are riding around with your picture on their dashboards looking for you?"

"Jake didn't recognize me. Besides, people see what they expect to see and no one is going to suspect Diana Kincaid of bringing home an escaped prisoner."

"They might when they see this truck." She struggled with the idea, sure it wouldn't work. "If my dad has someone watching the house, how do I explain the fact that I'm no longer pregnant?"

"You don't." He picked up the sack of food and lay it on her lap. "You can wad this bag and stuff it under your shirt. Once we're inside, pull all the shades and let them wonder what we're doing."

"Oh, they'll do more than wonder. The way my dad will huff and puff if he finds out what's going on, he'll make the big bad wolf look like he was only sneezing."

"Then I guess we're lucky your house isn't made of straw. It isn't, is it?"

"It's not going to work, Ross."

"Your place as headquarters, with clean clothes, running water and a bed. Or living out of this old pickup."

She swallowed hard. "You don't fight fair."

"I never said I did."

TRAVELING THE BACK ROADS was slow and indirect, and it was nearly dawn by the time they entered the city limits of Dallas. The streets were mostly deserted, the streetlights a glowing circle in a cloud of mist and smog.

Diana stretched her back and shoulders and gave her neck muscles a quick massage. Her tension level had increased significantly the closer they'd come to the city. One wrong move and Ross would be identified and arrested and she'd be left to conduct the search for Alexandra on her own. And now she felt increasing guilt that in helping her, he was significantly escalating his own problems.

It wasn't that she lacked confidence, but she didn't have the connections he did. He'd already found out about a baby-theft ring and gotten addresses of people for them to visit. "When can we call on the women whose names you have?"

"After daybreak. We can grab breakfast at your place and you can change clothes. Unfortunately, I have nothing else to change into, but at least these are clean."

Her place. She still thought it was a mistake, but she didn't have any better ideas. She gave Ross directions and a few minutes later, they were pulling into her driveway. She picked up the paper sack, now without the sandwiches, and wadded it into padding. Lifting her shirt, she fitted it inside, then pulled her shirt and jacket over it.

Ross scanned the area—twice. "I don't see anyone around."

"Still, we take no chances. My dad has only the best working for him. They can hide in keyholes."

"That would make privacy a little difficult."

"Try impossible."

She opened the door and climbed out. "I'll open the garage and you can pull the truck inside and out of sight."

"Good idea. I'm sure there are ordinances against leaving rubbish sitting in the driveway."

"In this neighborhood, there are ordinances against *having* rubbish."

Diana punched in the code that set the garage door in motion. It had been dark like this the last time she'd driven home. Dark and quiet. She'd parked the car, turned to get out, and that's when the tall man with eyes and hair as black as the night had jumped from the shadows. She'd screamed. She remembered the sound of it and the crunching footsteps as he'd dragged her into his car.

"Are you all right?" Ross was at her elbow, obviously sensing her fear.

"I'm okay." Only she wasn't. She wouldn't be until the men responsible were arrested and Alexandra was safe in her arms again.

ROSS FOLLOWED HER into the house, cautious, alert to any movement, any noise. He didn't want to alarm Diana, but he needed to check out every room, every place where a man could hide and wait. And it wasn't her father's spies he was concerned about.

"I'll make some hot chocolate," she said.

"Good idea." He checked the kitchen first since it was nearest the door they'd used to enter. Satisfied that it was all clear, he walked to the door that led into the dining room. "I'm going to walk through the house and make sure nothing looks as if the place were broken into."

"While you're looking, you can choose your guest room," she offered. "The one done in tan is the most masculine, but the one with the pink, lacy pillows and the antiques is the largest."

"A man doesn't need a lot of room to sleep." And he wouldn't be doing it on pink pillows if he could help it. But pink aside, the house was too rich for his blood. He liked simple things. Wood and leather and furniture you wouldn't be afraid to sit on.

Even the carpet made him nervous. Off-white, and not that far off. It made him think he should take his boots off and park them at the door, but he was too far inside to worry about that now. He checked the dining room and stepped into the foyer, peeking into the coat closet before wandering down a wide hall with paintings on either side. Real paintings. Not the paint-by-number variety or the prints you could buy already framed in the mall.

The first door off the hall was the master bedroom, the one Diana had undoubtedly shared with her husband before his death. The bed was king-size, covered in a striped spread in rich shades of brown, green and purple. He imagined them lying there together making love and the image grated along his nerve endings.

He was nuts to think about what her life had been like, or even to care. Even if she'd never had a husband, he wouldn't have a chance with her. Smart, sexy and rich, she could have her pick of men, and she wasn't likely to settle for a poor cowboy, at least not for more than a night. And he wasn't interested in having his heart bounced around like a basketball. He closed the door and went to the next room.

He regretted the move the second he opened the door. He regretted it all the more when Diana slipped in behind him. She crossed the room and turned the knob on a music box. Strains of a lullaby filled the nursery.

"Everything's ready for Alexandra," she whispered, turning and examining every detail as if she'd never seen them before. "I painted the room myself and I chose all the furniture and the fabrics for the curtains. No decorator. Just me."

"You did a good job."

She pushed the back of the rocker and set it in motion. "I tried out all the rockers in the store. I wanted one that fit just right so that I could hold my daughter for as long as she'd let me."

"You'll be rocking her in it before you know it." His words were no match for her sorrow, but it was all he had to offer.

She walked to the crib and picked up a plush teddy bear. "I used to sit in here at night and think about what it would be like after Alexandra was born. I'd hold the little bear in my arms and pretend it was Alexandra. But it was nothing like the real thing. They let me hold her a few times in the cabin where they held me captive. Did I tell you that?"

"You mentioned it."

"It wasn't like holding the lifeless toy at all. It was like holding a tiny, living miracle in my arms. And then Conan just walked over, took her from my arms and marched out the door." Her voice was hollow as if it came from some bottomless pit deep inside her.

"This isn't helping, Diana. I think we should go and get that chocolate you talked about."

She covered her eyes with her hands. "I know. I need to be tough."

"You are tough. You're just hurting. That's all. You wouldn't be human if you weren't." He wrapped an arm around her waist and she leaned her head against his shoulder. He stroked her hair, running his fingers through the dancing curls. He knew he shouldn't touch her at all, but he couldn't help himself.

He'd already let her get far closer to him than he'd let a woman in a long, long time. She was not for him, never would be. His mind knew that full well. But a man couldn't help the way he felt.

She pulled her head from his shoulder and looked him in the eyes. "I've changed my mind about the hot chocolate. I'm tired and I think I'll go and lie down."

"I recommend it. You can get in a few hours' sleep before we have to leave."

"Would you lie down beside me for a while."

"Lie down beside you, but don't touch you?" He shook his head. "I'd like to be that strong, but the truth is I'm not."

"Neither am I." She turned and held out a hand to him. "But lie down beside me anyway. I don't want to be alone right now."

"Not good enough. When I lie down beside you, it will be because you want *me,* not just a warm body."

"You're a strange man, Ross Taylor."

"You don't know the half of it."

He walked her back to her bedroom, then finished his inspection of the house. There were no signs of intruders, no signs of broken or picked locks. Satisfied that all was clear, he finally dropped onto the bed in the tan room.

In a matter of hours, they'd follow their two leads and hope they gave them something to go on. Every day Alexandra remained missing, the chances of finding

her alive grew smaller. He knew the statistics on these
things all too well.

He closed his eyes, but didn't have time to fall asleep
before the doorbell rang. He rushed to the window and
looked out, quickly spotting the squad car in the driveway.

The cops were on the scene.

# Chapter Eleven

Ross jumped up and raced down the hallway to Diana's room, a surge of adrenaline masking his fatigue. She was up and trying to pull on a robe, so panicked her arms were fighting the sleeves of the garment instead of sliding through them.

She stopped when she saw him. "It's the police, Ross! You have to hide. Climb into the attic and get behind the storage boxes or even in one. I'll stall them as long as I can." The words tumbled out of her mouth, ran into each other so that he could barely understand her.

He helped her with the robe, then took her hands in his. They were cold as ice. "I'm not going to hide. You're going to walk to the door and put on a nice little performance for the officers. Act as if you're surprised to see them. Assure them you're safe and send them on their way."

"It won't work. They know you're here, Ross."

The banging at the door grew louder. He had to work fast, calm Diana and jump-start her into action. He worked at keeping his voice calm. "There's no way for them to know I'm here. They don't have any reason to suspect that you've been anywhere near the area where I escaped from the sheriff.''

"Then why are they ringing my doorbell and banging on my door in the wee hours of the morning?''

"My guess would be that your parents asked them to check on you. Just open the door and convince them you're fine. Act sleepy and puzzled about why they're here.''

"If my dad had someone watching when we came in, they probably already know that I'm not alone.''

"If they ask, admit you have a guest. That's not a crime. Now go.'' He nudged her along. "Nice and easy. You can do it. I'll be right here.''

"But what if they insist on coming in?''

"Refuse them—nicely. I'm sure they don't have a search warrant and they can't just bust into your home without one. Now stay calm and do it. For Alexandra.''

The last comment did the trick. "I'll need this,'' she said, taking a pillow from the bed and stuffing it inside her robe. "Just in case they know I'm supposed to be pregnant.'' She took a deep breath and pulled the robe's belt tight, looping the ends into a bow as she started down the hall.

"I'm coming,'' she called, her voice so shaky it changed octaves three times on the two words.

He stayed in the bedroom, but kept the door ajar so that he could hear the interaction between Diana and the police officers who'd come calling on the governor's daughter in the darkness of night.

Hopefully he'd been right in assuming they weren't here because of him. But even if they were, it wasn't himself he was afraid for. There had been enough publicity about his escape now that he was sure the orders to the Halpern sheriff had been changed. It wasn't wise to shoot a prisoner that half the state of Texas knew about.

Ross's fears were for Diana. If he was arrested, she was just desperate enough to go up against Crowe alone, and Ross knew all too well what the man was capable of. That's why he had to see this thing through. He'd failed enough people in his life. He would not fail her.

"Is something the matter, Officer?"

Ross breathed a sigh of relief as he heard Diana speak. Somehow between the bedroom and the front door, she'd gotten it together. Her voice was slightly hoarse, as if she'd just wakened from a sound sleep. He waited and listened.

"Are you Diana Kincaid?"

"Yes, of course. This is my home. Is there a problem?"

"We were told to watch the house, see if we saw any sign of trouble."

"There's none that I'm aware of. I've been away for a few days, but everything seemed in place when I returned home an hour or so ago. Is there something I don't know?"

"You might want to call your mother."

"My mother. What's wrong? Has something happened?" Anxiety destroyed her attempt to stay calm, but even that should sound perfectly natural to the officer at the door.

"She was worried about you," he answered, his own voice calm. "Seems she got some weird phone call today and it upset her. Can't say as I blame her what with some fruitcake planting a bomb in the governor's office. And Kincaid's the best governor this state's ever seen.

But, just give your mother a call, and be sure to let her know we're on top of things."

"I'll do that."

"And I'm sorry we disturbed you, but we saw a light on that hadn't been on earlier and we decided it was best to check it out."

"I appreciate that. But as you can see, I'm fine. I went to the kitchen for water a little while ago and must have forgotten to switch the light off. I'm sorry my mother bothered you with this."

"Well, you know how moms are. No matter how old we get, they worry like we're teenagers. If I don't go by my mom's at least once a week, she gets all bent out of shape. No telling what she'd do if she got some sort of crank call saying I was in trouble." He flashed a broad smile.

Diana yawned loudly enough that Ross could hear her, evidently back on her performance. "Thanks for stopping by."

"Glad to be of service. If you need anything, give us a call. My partner and I are in the area all night."

Ross waited until he heard the door close and the squad car back out of the driveway before he walked down the hall to check on Diana. She was leaning against the front door, fingering the ties on her robe and staring into space.

"An Emmy-winning performance if ever I heard one."

"That's because you couldn't hear my heart beating from where you were standing." She splayed her hand against her chest. "It's still pounding."

"That's okay. Cops are vain. He probably thought it was his charm and good looks that had your heart pounding."

She smiled and loosened her robe enough for the pillow she'd used for stuffing to drop to the floor. The robe slit open, revealing a smattering of pink lace and a dip of cleavage. He forced himself to look away and wondered how long he would be able to handle seeing Diana night and day without ever finding any satisfaction for the urges that were tearing him apart.

"Did you hear everything?" she asked, turning to lock the dead bolt.

"I did. You impressed the heck out of me. Even the yawn sounded authentic."

"The officer who was doing the talking seemed to believe me, but the one standing on the walk kept looking behind him as if he thought someone was going to jump from the hedges."

"That's the job of the backup guy. Avoid surprises."

"How do you know so much about police work."

"I was a cop once, a long time ago."

"Why did you quit?"

"I didn't. I was fired."

She narrowed her eyes, and her expression changed in an instant. He knew without her saying it that a shadow of doubt had crept into her mind. He couldn't blame her. All she really knew about him was that he'd showed up in handcuffs and that he was wanted for murdering a rancher in Halpern, Texas.

"Why were you fired?"

"It's a long story, one we can easily save for another night. But I didn't kill anybody, if that's what you're worried about. I just took my work too personally. At least that's how my supervisor put it when he handed me my walking papers."

She nodded. "I can believe that."

Her voice dropped to a murmur, became intimate,

seductive. Their gazes locked, and he wondered if a kiss had ever affected him as much as the flash of desire he saw mirrored in the emerald green of her eyes.

She stepped toward him. "You take protecting me personally, and you hardly know me."

"Just another of my faults."

She kept coming, stopping so near it would have been difficult to pass a pencil between them. He ached to reach out to her, take her mouth with his, taste her, mingle their breaths. But he would never be able to stop with a kiss. And once they passed that line from friends and partners to lovers, nothing would ever be the same. At least, it wouldn't for him. He took a deep breath and walked to the kitchen.

"*I* need a drink of water," he said. A nice, cold one. "*You* need to call your mother, let her know that you're all right."

She followed him to the kitchen, but didn't look his way. The moment had passed. He'd dodged the bullet. Too bad he didn't feel better for it.

"I'll wait until the sun comes up." She opened the cabinet door and chose two tall glasses, real glass, not the plastic ones he'd had in his apartment—back when he'd had an apartment.

"If your mother's worried enough to call the police, she's probably not sleeping soundly anyway. Tell her the cops came by and mentioned the phone call she received today. Find out what the man said that upset her so much."

Diana whirled around to face him. "The phone call. I'd almost forgotten. You don't think it could be the men who have Alexandra, do you?"

"I guess there's only one way to find out."

She grabbed the phone and Ross had never seen anyone punch in a set of numbers so fast.

DIANA WAITED as the phone at her parents' house rang for what seemed like an interminable amount of time. She dreaded talking to her mother, not because they weren't close, but because they were. The relationship between them had been strained at times, especially during Diana's college years when she'd did everything she could to separate herself from the fishbowl-type existence that characterized the lives of Texas politicians and their families.

But once Diana had married Alex Hastings, an up-and-coming surgeon of whom both her parents approved, she and her mother had become closer than ever. And her father had been greatly relieved to turn the responsibility for her over to her new husband.

"Hello."

"Hi, Mom."

"Diana!"

She could hear the relief in her mother's voice. "I'm sorry to wake you at this time of the morning."

"You didn't. I wasn't asleep. I've been so worried about you."

"Didn't Dad tell you I'd called."

"Yes, but that didn't keep me from worrying. Not with the baby due in less than two weeks. Where are you?"

"I'm home now. I visited a friend's lake house for a few days. I was growing too impatient just waiting, but I didn't mean for you to worry. I asked Dad to tell you that I was fine."

"He told me, but I was still afraid something had happened to you and if it had, I just—"

Her mother's voice broke and Diana could hear her sniffling over the wire. She could also hear her father in the background, wanting to know who was on the phone and what in Sam Hill was wrong now.

"Nothing's wrong, dear. It's Diana. She's home and—oh, Diana, you're not in labor, are you?" The strain in her voice picked up a thread of excitement.

"Not yet." Lies begat lies, and with every one Diana told, the web of deception she was spinning grew larger. *For a good cause,* she reminded herself as the guilt settled like dumbbells on her chest. "I had two policemen come by the house a minute ago."

"Oh, dear. I hope they didn't upset you."

"No, but they said something about a phone call you'd received."

"Oh, that. I don't know what the world's coming to."

"Exactly what did the man say?"

"It's too horrible to even repeat. Let's just forget it since you and the baby are both fine."

"Did he say something about my baby?" She hated to keep pushing but she had to know.

"Yes, but it was just crazy. He said to tell you that your daughter was crying for you."

Diana dropped to one of the straight-backed chairs, her legs rubbery, her insides a quaking mass of nerves. "Did he say anything else?"

"No, that was all. Diana, you just don't sound like yourself. Are you sure the doctor didn't find anything wrong with the baby when you went for your checkup?"

"No. He said, 'All systems go.'" The words that Doc had spoken while Alexandra was pushing her way from the womb echoed in Diana's mind, and dread grew so real she could taste it. Somehow she got through the rest of the conversation. When she hung up the phone she repeated the message to Ross.

"What do you think it means?" she asked, her insides shaking so badly she could barely talk. "They told me I'd never see Alexandra again, so why would they call my mother and leave a message like that?"

"I wish I knew. Maybe they were just hoping to find out if you were there."

She leaned her elbows on the table and buried her head in her hands. "I can't imagine that the mob deals in slow torture. I thought they specialized in quick hits. Gun them down and move on."

Ross took the rest of his water and poured it into the sink with such vengeance that the water sloshed over the sides and splattered over the counter. "Don't kid yourself, Diana. The mob does whatever J. B. Crowe orders."

"But I've seen Crowe. He appears so normal, a little classy, actually."

"A front. He walks around in expensive suits, eats in the finest restaurants, goes to church with his family. He never gets his hands dirty. He doesn't have to. He just gives an order and his paid assassins jump to do his bidding."

Ross's words had turned to granite—cold, sharp, bitter. When Diana looked up, it was as if the weight of the world had crawled onto his shoulders and drawn battle lines in his face.

She hugged her arms about herself, fighting off a chill not connected to the temperature. "How do you know so much about J. B. Crowe?"

"Because my brother was one of his assassins."

DIANA WAS STARING at him as if he'd just landed from Mars. He looked away, paced the room, then walked back to lean against the kitchen counter. He hadn't intended to blurt out the truth, but the old hatred had sprung back to life this week, consuming him, destroying that veneer of pretense that had let him believe he'd moved past it.

"You said *was*. Where's your brother now?"

"Six feet under."

"I'm sorry."

"It's not your fault. I wish I could say the same for myself."

"Surely you didn't shoot him."

"No, but I stayed on his case until I finally convinced him to turn state's evidence and go into a witness protection program. But once again Crowe came out on top. Somehow he found out where Ralph was being kept. He was killed before he ever got to testify."

Diana stretched her hands across the counter and covered his. For once her touch didn't set him on fire. He took it for what it was, an expression of empathy.

"Is that when you became a cop?"

"No, I was already a cop, just like my dad before me, only instead of working as sheriff in one of the state's rural areas, I worked the streets of Dallas."

She walked around the counter to stand beside him. "It must have crushed your dad to find out his son was involved with Crowe and then see him killed when he tried to right the wrong he'd done."

"It did more than crush him. It destroyed him. He went gunning for Crowe himself, rushed right into a trap and took a bullet to the heart. All the family I had left, lost to J. B. Crowe in a matter of days."

"Oh, Ross. I'm so sorry." She slipped into his arms.

He held her, knowing he should have never let her see inside him, glimpse the loss that still drove him, made him the loner he'd become.

She didn't ask for the sordid details. She was first class all the way. But since he'd started, he may as well finish the story. "I used my position on the force to go after Crowe. He claimed I was harassing him, which I was. Eventually I was fired for taking my job too personally and Crowe was left to run the mob. For the last year, I've wandered around the country, picking up odd jobs whenever I could. A month ago I decided I was ready to move back to Texas. And here I am."

"I'm glad," she said. "I'm sorry for your heartache, sorry for the reasons that brought us together, but I'm still glad you're here."

"And that may be the nicest thing a beautiful woman's ever said to me." He drew away, suddenly so tired he wasn't sure he could make it back to the bedroom if he didn't go now.

"Get some sleep," he said, pausing to lay a hand on her shoulder as he passed. "The sun's already sending the first golden glow over the horizon and we have a full day in front of us."

"I know, but I was just thinking. Wouldn't it be something if by finding Alexandra, we're the ones to bring Crowe down?"

He nodded. "It would be something, all right. But don't expect it. The man's untouchable." Only Ross didn't really believe that. Someday, someway, J. B. Crowe would get what he had coming to him. With any luck, Ross would be around to watch it happen.

But Diana was no match for the man, and he would not lose anyone else he cared about to Crowe. Never.

Not even if he had to kill the man in cold blood first just to stop him.

## DAY 7

DIANA SIPPED her coffee cautiously from the go-cup as Ross guided her red BMW through the early-morning traffic. "At this rate, we'd make better time jogging," she said, "not that I'm suggesting we try it."

"Why not? I'm up for it."

"Not me, but I am impatient and more than a little anxious about these interviews today."

He reached over and patted her hand reassuringly. "This is no time to lose your optimism."

"I'm still optimistic about finding Alexandra. I just hope we're not chasing bubbles today. We don't have time to waste."

"At least we're doing something positive. If the first woman we're going to see describes one of the men who abducted you or the one who kidnapped you at your house as the man who talked to her about selling her baby, we'll know we're on the right track."

She ran her fingers along the edge of her seat belt, still troubled by what Ross had told her last night about his brother and his father. "I'm convinced Crowe's a hard and powerful man after what you told me last night, but it seems strange that he would become involved in something like baby smuggling. Drugs, money laundering, extortion. It seems that would be enough to line his pockets."

"Crime is big business. They diversify. And the mob isn't one man. Crowe's just the head, the CEO so to speak. And this sounds just like him. Steal Thomas Kincaid's granddaughter and sell her for a profit. The ultimate revenge.''

Ross threw on the brake, bringing the car to a jolting stop as I-20 traffic came to an abrupt standstill. Diana held her coffee out in front of her, thankful the thick, curved rim kept the black liquid from sloshing onto the floor and her brown slacks. She had worn a carefully placed throw pillow under a raincoat until she'd gotten into the car, but she'd thrown both coat and pillow into the back seat once they'd gotten under way.

A squad car passed them, sirens blaring and lights flashing. She glanced around, half expecting them to be surrounded by police. ''This is just too bizarre. That officer just drove right by you without a glance. Yet every cop on the road has probably looked at your picture this morning.''

''It's not unusual at all. People tend to see what they expect to see. It's one of the first things you learn when you start questioning witnesses at the scene of a crime or an accident. In our case the authorities are looking for an itinerant cowboy on the run. They're not looking for me in Diana Kincaid's BMW.''

''So that's why you tossed your cowboy hat in the back seat when you climbed into the car.''

''I thought I'd try to play the part of a typical commuter.''

''You dress like a cowboy and you call yourself a cowboy,'' she said, ''but the only job I've heard you mention is that of a cop.''

''My mom died shortly after my brother was born and Dad took us back to live with my grandparents on their ranch. While Dad worked for the sheriff's department, I followed my Grandpa's every step. I was riding before I started school and barrel racing before I could read."

"Preschool rodeo star. I bet you stole all the little cowgirls' hearts."

"Yeah, buddy." He exaggerated his Texas drawl and flashed a teasing smile. The smile altered his features, made him look years younger than the strained expression she'd gotten used to over the past few days.

Not that he had a lot of reason to smile. His own hell was still waiting for him when this was over, if he managed to avoid arrest that long. He was quite a man, different from any she'd ever known, though she'd been around cowboys all her life. When she was younger, her family had spent lots of time on the Kincaid ranch just west of Dallas.

But as her father had started to climb the rungs of political success, he'd left more and more of the ranch responsibilities to a paid foreman and spent his time commuting between his home in Dallas and the capitol in Austin.

She still went to the ranch occasionally, mostly when she felt the need to ride a fast horse and feel the wind in her face. But if she'd run into a cowboy like Ross there, she'd probably have gone a lot more often. It was amazing that some woman hadn't realized what a special man he was and put a ring on his finger long before now. Or maybe someone had...

"Have you ever been married, Ross?"

"No. Never found a woman who'd have me—at least not one that I'd have. Most women want money, a big house in the suburbs, a man who goes to work with a choking tie around his neck. I'd only disappoint them."

"You're much too hard on yourself. Surely you want a wife and children someday."

"Someday. If it works out that way."

He stared straight ahead, but she could sense that her questions were making him uncomfortable. Men and emotions. They expressed them in a thousand ways—but almost never in words.

"How'd you meet your late husband?" he asked, probably more to change the subject than out of curiosity.

"I had just started med school, but wasn't at all sure that I had really wanted to be a doctor. He was a fourth-year medical student, dedicated and determined to become the best surgeon in all of Texas if not the world."

"I'm surprised he had time to date."

"He didn't, but when we were together, he was gentle and loving. He swept me right off my feet, much to the delight of my parents who'd been sure up until then that I was going to run away with the first man who could party heartier than I could."

"But you were willing to give up partying for a serious man?"

"I was willing to give up everything for Alex, but I never felt as if I'd given up one iota. Though, I was lonely sometimes after we married. The stress of having people's lives in his hands on an almost daily basis not only kept him away from home a lot but frequently made him draw inside himself. In the last years he spent more and more of his at-home time with his books and journals."

"But you must have both wanted a baby."

"Probably me more than him, but he was totally supportive. He went through a myriad of tests and fertility treatments with me and hardly ever took time to do anything just for himself. That's why I was thrilled when he finally agreed to go with Dad on a fishing trip in the Gulf of Mexico. His last trip anywhere.'' The old familiar heaviness settled in her chest as the memories rushed into her mind and numbed her senses.

''You don't have to tell me any of this.''

''I know, but I want to.'' And strangely enough she did. Maybe because he was so easy to talk to, or maybe she felt she owed him an explanation of who she really was and what her life had been. ''The boat got caught in a freak storm. They radioed for help from the Coast Guard but before the rescue team could arrive, the boat sank. My father managed to secure a life jacket and stay afloat until help arrived. Alex's body was never found.''

Ross said nothing, but he reached over and took her hand in his. She held it, for once not feeling guilty, just thankful that he was with her. She'd loved Alex dearly, but he would never be coming back. Ross was here, and no matter what the future held, she'd never be sorry that she'd asked him to help her find her baby. Never be sorry that she'd invited him into her life.

She only hoped that by doing so she'd not brought him a guilty verdict when he went to trial for the murder of Darrell Arnold.

''YOU'RE AWFULLY QUIET over there. Is my driving scaring you into submission?''

''Your driving's fine.''

''Good. I could get used to handling a car like this. Next to my horse, it's the best ride I've had in a long time.''

''You don't have a horse.''

''Sure I do. All cowboys have a horse. It's one of the requirements.''

''Like being able to sense concrete two miles before you can see it.''

"You got it."

"So, where is this horse?"

"Whiskey's at my granddad's ranch. Well, actually, Grandpa's dead and it's my ranch now, though I haven't been back there for over a year."

"Who takes care of things?"

"I leased it out to one of the neighbors. But he promised to take care of my horse for me. The poor animal's probably pining away for me as we speak."

"No doubt." She recognized Ross's tactics, knew he was concerned that she'd grown quiet and withdrawn. The cowboy beside her was an amazing man. She leaned her head against the backrest and closed her eyes, letting the truth of her feelings for him tiptoe around the edge of her consciousness. She liked him way too much.

The traffic started moving again, and she forced her mind away from Ross and toward the woman they were going to see. All she needed was one scrap of information, one seemingly insignificant fact that would lead them to Alexandra. It would happen. She couldn't go on unless she believed that.

She prayed this would be the day.

J. B. CROWE SAT DOWN at the square table and waited for his two top men. The café was one of his favorites, a mom-and-pop establishment in the neighborhood where he'd grown up. He and Thomas Kincaid.

It was a perfect place for a meeting like the one he'd called for this morning. No bugs built into the salt shakers. No cops hiding in the kitchen.

A perfect place for him and his men, but not nearly nice enough for his daughter Amanda or his new granddaughter. He still couldn't believe that Amanda had threatened to walk out of his life completely if he didn't drop all his connections with the mob. She was his baby, his princess, the light of his life and she'd always been. He couldn't imagine waking up every day knowing he'd never see her again.

But she was headstrong enough to make good on her threat if she thought he was going back on his word to turn over a new law-abiding leaf. That's why he had to be careful for a while, keep a low profile, not let Thomas Kincaid know that he'd been behind Diana's kidnapping.

Thomas Kincaid. As usual, the root of all his problems. If the man hadn't started his extremely vocal crusade to rid Texas of organized crime, Amanda wouldn't even know there was a mob, much less that he was the kingpin. He'd always been a businessman in her mind, and he had to make sure she saw him that way again.

He looked up as the two men he'd been waiting for walked through the door, waved and started toward him. He greeted them and made small talk until the coffee was served, until everyone had started to relax. That was his way. Hit when the enemy least expected it. Not that these men were his enemies, or at least he hoped they weren't. But he knew they were thinking that he was growing soft, that he couldn't even rule his own family anymore. He'd let his daughter become involved with an ex-cop who'd tried to infiltrate the Crowe organization.

Only he hadn't *let* his daughter do anything. But even though she'd dishonored him, he'd protect her with his life. And if this traitor was what it took to make her happy, then he'd protect him, too. But heaven help the man if he ever broke Amanda's heart.

He took a long sip of coffee, then placed his cup back

on the table. He had to make a strong move, prove that he was the man he'd always been even though he'd promised his daughter he'd walk away from the mob. Prove that he would not be run over by Thomas Kincaid. He cleared his throat and the men looked up expectantly.

"I guess you all know by now that not only did Ross Taylor kill Darrell Arnold and then escape the Halpern sheriff, but he was the one who broke into the cabin while Doc neglected his duties. He and Diana Kincaid are together somewhere and I can only guess what they're up to."

"Looking for Diana's baby I bet," the man to his right said. "But they won't find her."

"No, thanks to more mistakes on our part." Crowe spread his hands on the table. "I want Ross Taylor found before another day is through. Once he's out of the picture and no longer agitating things, Diana Kincaid will go running to her father."

"Does that mean you want Ross Taylor killed?"

"Is that what I said?"

"No, but—"

"No more buts. No more mistakes. No more excuses. And if I find out that one of you pulled that stupid bomb stunt in the governor's office, I'll personally take care of him."

"So are we supposed to just take that man's flak? He's blabbing to every newspaper and television station in town that he's going to squash us like bugs. And he's using our real names now. I wouldn't be surprised if he has a plant somewhere in our top echelons."

"Don't worry about Thomas Kincaid. He falls in my department. As will Ross Taylor once he's in my hands. Now are there any questions?"

The men all shook their heads. Crowe motioned to the young waiter to come and take their breakfast order. The meeting was over. The next move would be between him and Ross Taylor. He should have killed the troublemaker eighteen months ago when he took out the rest of his family.

A mistake that would be remedied in a matter of hours.

## Chapter Twelve

The BMW looked out of place in the dirt drive, its lines too sleek for the clumps of weeds that bordered the path, its paint too shiny for the drabness of the small clapboard house that sat in a jungle of untended lawn. Empty beer cans were scattered across the porch and an upside down plastic cooler leaned against a broken lawn chair.

"Not the neatest people in the world," Ross said, as Diana met him in front of the car.

"But at least the woman said no when someone offered her money to sell her baby. Not only that, but apparently she had the nerve to report the offer to the police."

Ross tapped his knuckles against the door. A few minutes later it opened a crack, and a burly guy in a stained T-shirt poked his head out. "Whatever you're selling, we ain't buying."

Diana's confidence took a mind-numbing plunge. She couldn't imagine this man answering their questions, but she could picture him aiming a shotgun in their faces and ordering them off the premises.

"We're not selling anything," Ross answered. "We're looking for some information."

"What kind of information?"

"I heard there was some creep going around trying to get women to sell their babies to him," he said, talking a language the man would understand and not feel as if they were talking down to him. "I'd like to find him, show him we don't put up with that kind of business around here."

"You a cop?"

"No."

"Then I don't know nothing."

"Well maybe we could talk to your wife? Is she here?"

"Yeah." He turned away from them. "Come in here a minute, Leigh. These folks want to ask you something."

*Talk, Leigh. Cooperate. Tell me something that will help me find Alexandra.*

But the moment the woman stepped into view, Diana knew that wasn't likely to happen. She was no more than twenty, at least fifteen years younger than her husband. Anorexic thin, her skin looked almost transparent and a spot on her right cheek was colored a sickly shade of purple.

Diana swallowed and dived in, hoping Leigh might feel more comfortable answering a woman's questions. "I heard you have a new baby."

"No." Her voice was thin and cracked, like a wafer that had been left out to dry. "You heard wrong."

"But you made a formal complaint that someone had come here wanting to buy your baby."

The man put his hand around her shoulders and pulled her against his sweaty body. "She told you. She don't have no baby. You've got the wrong people."

The man started to shut the door, but Diana stuck a

foot inside and stood her ground. "Please, Leigh, as one mother to another, I have to know about these men. Just tell me what they looked like."

The man pushed in front of his wife. "You don't hear too well, lady. No men. No baby. You got that?"

She got it, and the truth of it turned her inside out. There was no baby because the brute in the dirty undershirt had *persuaded* the woman to change her mind about selling her child. The bruises were there for the world to see, but Diana was certain that the worst scars were hidden deep inside the woman's soul.

She wanted to grab her by the shoulders and shake sense into her. Tell her there were places for battered women to go for help, make her see that no man in the world was worth selling your child for.

Mostly, she ached for herself and seethed with rage toward the man who stood in the door glaring at her, daring her to start something.

"No men. No baby." This time the words came from Ross, slow, deliberate. "I guess we can live with that, if you can." He put an arm across Diana's shoulders and led her down the steps and back to the BMW.

"She sold her baby," she said, as Ross turned from the driveway onto the back road that had brought them to this place. "She gave in to that slob and sold her baby."

"It looks that way."

She slammed a fist into his shoulder as tears burned behind her eyelids. "Don't just act as if it's nothing, Ross Taylor. I was depending on her. I needed to know what they told her, how they made contact, if they'll be back. I need *something*."

Ross slowed the car and pulled off onto the shoulder, stopping clear of the roadway. He grabbed her fist and cuddled it between his two hands. "It's one dead end, Diana. That's all. You can't bang your head up against it. You just have to find another way to get the information you need."

She pushed her forehead into the spot on his shoulder that she'd just pelted with her fist. "Right now I think I could strangle J. B. Crowe with my bare hands. Him and every flunky he has in his damned organization."

"That's the spirit."

He tangled his fingers in her hair and she ached to crawl into his arms. Frustration, anger, heartbreak, desire. They collided, became one giant overwhelming surge of emotion.

She looked up and her gaze found and locked with Ross's. They were separated by inches of space and miles of differences. Right now, the differences just didn't matter. She stretched toward him, closed her eyes and kissed him.

ROSS HESITATED at first, afraid to feel what he knew was coming. But Diana's lips were too soft, too pliant, salty sweet from the tears that had squeezed from her eyes. He circled her with his arms, pulling her close. She melted into him, the soft curves of her breasts fitting themselves against the hard planes of his chest.

The desire he'd tried to stamp into oblivion over the past few days surfaced full-blown. He probed, kissed too hungrily, sucked her breath into his and still he couldn't get enough. His hand roamed her back and his tongue plundered her mouth while every breath-stealing sensation he'd ever felt rocked through him.

Finally, she pulled away. "I shouldn't have done that," she said, her voice raspy, her lips swollen from his kisses.

"You're right. You shouldn't have. I knew we wouldn't like it."

She smiled, but still she scooted back to her side of the car. He turned the key in the ignition and pulled back onto the highway. Neither of them spoke, but the air between them sizzled with an awareness so palpable he figured it had to take up space. And he wondered how he'd make it through the day without kissing her again.

DYLAN GARRETT SAT across the table from Zach Logan. The man hadn't changed all that much since Dylan first started working for him not long out of college. He was probably in his fifties now, but he'd always seemed wise beyond his years. His black hair was still thick though it had receded a little along the forehead and his mustache perpetually needed a good trimming with a sharp pair of scissors.

Zach reached in his pocket for a package of antacids. He worked a couple loose with his fingertips and popped them into his mouth.

Dylan stretched his legs toward Zach's cluttered desk. "Still eating those things like candy, I see."

"I missed my lunch."

"You're going to miss your stomach, too, when it's gone."

"Nah. I won't live long enough for that to happen. My wife's going to kill me first."

"Is she on you to retire again?"

"This time it's just a vacation she's after. Wants to take one of those cruises where you sit around on the deck of some swanky ship and watch the women walk by in bikinis. Not that she mentioned that part of the itinerary."

"You should try it. Fun might agree with you, let you stop popping those pills."

"I will, just as soon as J. B. Crowe's behind bars. Governor Kincaid says it's going to happen and after all my years of trying to catch him, I'd hate to be off vacationing when it does."

Zach picked up a stack of papers from the corner of his desk. He rippled through them to show Dylan how many there were and then plopped them back on his desk. "This is what we've collected on Crowe and the mob over the years." He made a circle with his thumb and index finger and held it in front of him. "This is what we've made stick."

"You don't have to tell me. I was in the pit with him, remember. I drank his wine, ate his food, could have slept with some of his women if I'd been of a mind to. Not his wife, of course, and definitely not his daughter, but any of the others."

"But that's exactly what my last undercover man did. I heard from Jesse Brock today. He's with Amanda Crowe right now and she's told her father that they're getting married. She also told her dad that unless he gives up his mob connections, she won't let him be part of her or his granddaughter's life."

"You've got to be kidding me, Zach. Crowe will never let his daughter marry a cop, especially one who went undercover right beneath Crowe's nose."

"Apparently Amanda Crowe believes he will. Of course, Jesse's actually an ex-cop now. You can't sleep with the enemy's daughter and stay on the force."

"I guess even Crowe has a soft spot when it comes to his own flesh and blood."

"At least when it comes to Amanda. According to

Jesse, Crowe told her he'd do whatever it takes to keep her on speaking terms with him.''

"You don't believe that, do you?"

"No, and neither does Jesse. That's why I'm especially glad you agreed to come back and help us out. I don't know what's going on, but like I told you yesterday, Kincaid's got his own task force working overtime to get something that will put Crowe down for good. And you know J.B.'s not just going to sit by and let Kincaid arrest him. As far as I'm concerned he's the man behind that bomb threat in Kincaid's office.''

"The governor's in Austin. You can leave that worry to their police department.''

"But Crowe's in Dallas and so is Kincaid's daughter. Mrs. Kincaid called the department yesterday saying someone called her saying strange things about Diana. And now that it's over, Kincaid admitted to me that just last week someone called him and claimed to have kidnapped Diana.''

"Have you talked to Diana?"

"No, but the pair that patrol her neighborhood saw a light in one of her rooms just before daylight this morning. They stopped in and reported back that she said there were no problems.''

"So what do you have on my schedule for the day?"

"Talk to me. I need your knowledge of how Crowe's operation works. You know, the threats, the intimidation. I need you to help me second-guess him so that I'm ready for whatever he throws at us.''

"I'm just here temporarily. Don't forget it." Dylan crossed an ankle over his knee.

"Then let's get down to business. I guess you heard about your old buddy Ross Taylor being arrested on murder charges over in Halpern and then escaping from the sheriff while he was being transported to another jail.''

"I heard.''

"Did you also hear that he was with a woman?''

"Yeah. So what are you getting at?''

"I think the woman he's with could be Diana Kincaid.''

"Why would you think that?''

"The description we got from the two kids whose truck they stole fits her perfectly. And one of Diana's neighbors called into the department claiming she saw Diana Kincaid leave her house this morning with a man who fit Ross Taylor's description. I know it sounds crazy, but so do half the tips we get and a few of them actually turn out to be accurate.''

"Diana Kincaid wouldn't have a new baby, would she?''

"No. She's pregnant. Due any day. I don't know what's going on, but Ross is wanted for murder. If he shows up at Diana Kincaid's house tonight, I'll have to arrest him.''

"Due any day, uh?'' Dylan knew what he had to do but it didn't make it a bit easier. Ratting on a friend who'd trusted you was never easy. But lives were at stake. He had no choice.

Zach picked up a pencil and scribbled down a few lines. "I just wish I had a clue as to what Diana Kincaid and Ross Taylor would be doing together.''

"I think I can answer that question for you, Zach.'' It might have been the first time he'd ever seen his old boss look totally surprised.

DIANA HAD A nagging pain in her right temple as they drove back into the city. Their second house call had been as fruitless as the first. This time they had visited a polite, exceptionally neat grandmother. A few weeks ago she'd reported to the police that she feared her daughter who was seriously addicted to crack cocaine had sold her newborn to pay for her drug habit.

Now, the mother insisted her daughter had only given it up for adoption. She wouldn't say any more, but she'd been nervous and eager for them to leave. It was clear that someone had convinced her to keep her mouth shut. Diana had no doubts who that someone worked for, or what kind of threats they'd made to get their point across. She was as certain now as Ross that there was actually a black-market baby ring and that it was the work of the Texas mafia.

"I can't take this anymore," she said, no longer trying to hide her desperation. "I'm ready to go to Crowe. I'll get on my hands and knees and beg. I'll do anything. I just want my daughter back."

"If I thought that would help, I'd drive you over."

"What will help, Ross?"

"You could go to the police."

"The mob have been flaunting their crimes in the face of the police for years. They haven't made a dent in the organization, at least that's what my father says and now I believe him."

"And all for money."

"Money! That's it, Ross! We've been going at this all wrong."

He turned toward her, his brows arched. "I'm not following."

"We've been trying to talk to the women who've sold their babies or to their families. These are the people Crowe has power over, the ones he's using. We need to go for the buyers, the ones with money, the ones he's courting."

"Buying babies is still illegal. These people aren't going to risk going to jail and losing the babies to talk to you."

"No, we have to get to them first, before the child is actually in their hands. Find women who are not only rich, or at least well off, but who are also desperate to have a baby. That must be what the mob does."

"Women who are rich can go through legal channels to adopt a child."

"Not everyone can. A lot of people don't meet the requirements. Sometimes it's age, or health or something in their past that makes them a poor risk. And a legal adoption can sometimes take years. Some women don't want to wait that long."

"Women who are desperate for a baby. I doubt they belong to a club or a chat line. I don't know how you'd even begin to identify them."

"But these are the women who Crowe's targeting. He finds them, so there has to be a way to do it. And when we do, at least some of them should be willing to tell us if they've been approached by black-market sellers."

He frowned, obviously still dubious. "It would take months to get the sample you're talking about."

She pulled her legs into the seat with her, her headache gone now that her mind had something positive to concentrate on. "Any adoption agency would have a list of rejects. They'd have a file on the people as well, personal information."

"They might, but those records are confidential. They don't even release them to police without a search warrant and you'd need concrete evidence to get a search warrant for something like that."

"I can't wait that long anyway. My mother will be back in Dallas any day to be with me when she thinks I should be going into labor. Once she realizes I've had my baby and that her granddaughter is missing, everything will be out of my hands and into Dad's. And at this point, I'm sure even he would turn it over to the police."

"Which is probably the best solution for you as well."

But she couldn't let it go. The mob had to find buyers for the babies. Even if they got their clients by word of mouth, someone had to know about them—someone who would talk. All she had to do was find those people. Or get them to find her. "That's it! We'll get the right people to find us."

Ross cast a quick glance her way. "Something in the way you say that makes me think I'm not going to agree with whatever's going on in your pretty little head."

"I'm going to run an ad in the Sunday paper suggesting I can help people who've been turned down by other adoption agencies. When they call, I'll ask questions designed to find out if they've been offered the opportunity to buy a baby illegally. If they have, I'll persuade them to tell me who contacted them and how."

"It's already Thursday. I doubt you can even make the deadline for Sunday's paper."

"Then I'll run it Monday."

"This idea is so far in the back pasture, you can't even get a horse to it."

"Do you have a better idea?"

"No." He reached across the seat and took her hand.

"Even if by some wild fluke, we manage to find the men who run the baby-smuggling operation, it doesn't guarantee that we'll be able to track down your daughter."

"But we'll have a better chance at it than we do now. The men will go to jail and there will be no reason for them not to talk, to cooperate in hopes it will reduce their sentence."

"No reason unless you count retaliation by Crowe."

"With any luck, we'll implicate him as well."

"You are an optimist, Diana Kincaid."

"Always." Her mind was in a whirl the rest of the way home. It was a long shot, but it could work. And right now, it was her best option. If it didn't work then she might have to go to the authorities. But, in her mind, that would be the same as giving up.

In the meantime, Ross was still wanted by the police, and she knew that every minute he stayed free was a phenomenon in itself. He exited the Interstate and turned down the street that led to her subdivision. A police siren sounded in the distance, and she was hit with a twinge of anxiety, knowing that sooner or later someone would find him.

"Do you think it's safe for you to stay at my house again tonight?"

"No reason to run yet."

He reached the corner, turning onto her street. When he slowed, she looked up from the notes she was scribbling on the back of an envelope she'd found in her purse. Her mouth flew open as she stared at the four police cars parked in and out of her drive. One cop was striding around the side of her house, gun drawn. Another was holding a bull horn.

"Okay, Diana. Now it's time to run."

DIANA STOOD just inside the door, examining the motel room. It was small, a bed with a table on either side and a simple chest with two drawers and a cubbyhole that housed a seventeen-inch TV. It was clean, and that was about the best thing she could say for it.

They hadn't chosen it for the amenities but for the location. It was tucked away in an old section of town, not near any major highways and the parking area was hidden from the street by a wooden privacy fence. Ross had stayed out of sight while she'd registered as Mrs. James Donovan and paid in cash.

"A different bed every night," Diana quipped. "My reputation will be as bad as it was during my college days."

Ross walked to the window and pulled the curtains, shutting out the late-afternoon sun and the view of the trash Dumpster at the back of the building. "You talk a good story, but I have trouble believing you were as wild as you say."

"You're right. I dressed the part, lots of leather and bangles, but I was more illusion than reality. Still, my dad bought it, and a few of my dates—until they started to get fresh."

"Don't forget the man who gave you the tattoo."

She smiled. "That intrigues you, doesn't it."

"*You* intrigue me."

"That's only because you don't really know me. When I'm not caught up in the middle of a crime wave, I lead a rather boring, predictable life."

"You're Governor Kincaid's daughter. That puts you in a pretty elite group."

"My dad's the governor, not me. He thrives on power and action, on being in the limelight."

"And what do you thrive on, Diana?"

He walked up behind her and put his hands at her waist. She turned to face him, and the nearness of him consumed her.

"I thrived on the life that was growing inside me. What about you, Ross Taylor? What do you thrive on?"

"I didn't thrive at all. Not until I busted through the door of that cabin the other day." He trailed a finger down her face, from her forehead, over her nose, to her lips.

She parted them and took his fingertip into her mouth, sucking gently. Her world was falling apart, and yet the kiss this afternoon had broken down barriers. She could no longer deny that she wanted his touch and ached to kiss him again. She'd never expected to feel this way about a man again, but she did.

"Do you have any idea how badly I want to make love with you?" he whispered.

"I think so. And I want you. But I can't, not the way a man and a woman usually make love. It hasn't been long enough since I gave birth."

"I'd never want to hurt you."

"Then just lie beside me and touch me, Ross. Touch me in all the places that a man touches a woman when he wants her."

He cradled her face in his hands and kissed her, gently, more of a question than a statement. "I have nothing to offer you when this is over, Diana. I'll be arrested. I'll have a trial to face."

"Then we'll have to settle for now." She took his hand and led him toward the bed.

# Chapter Thirteen

Ross fumbled with the buttons on Diana's blouse. He was as awkward as if it were his first time, and in a way it was. It was the first time he'd ever made love to a woman who'd totally captured his heart. There were things he should say, but even if he knew the right words, he doubted he could make them come out right.

His emotions were raw, his body on fire. Finally, she helped him out, loosening the last two buttons herself and throwing her blouse to the floor. Seconds later, she'd unzipped her slacks and let them slide down her long legs. He picked her up and lay her in the middle of the bed, and she took his mouth hungrily. It was long minutes before he pulled away and shed his own clothes.

"I'm not sure how to do this," he said, stretching out beside her. "I don't want to hurt you."

She took his hand and laid it on her abdomen. "Touch me, Ross." She slid his hand to her bra-covered breasts and then down to the lacy border of her silky panties. "Make me feel beautiful. Make me feel loved. Give me a moment where I think of nothing but you and me and the need that burns inside us."

He stroked her, his fingers sliding over the naked flesh. "I can't believe this feels so right."

"It is right, Ross. And it's the only thing I have in my life right now that is."

She kissed him again, less hungrily, but twice as sweet. He reached behind her back and unclasped her bra. It fell loose and her breasts spilled out and onto his chest. With a groan, he broke away from the kiss to stare at the perfect mounds and the full nipples. "You're beautiful," he whispered. "All of you."

"My figure's not back to normal yet."

"Beauty isn't a pinup girl in a men's magazine. It's a real woman, full grown, full of love. And you are beautiful." He cupped her breasts, one at a time, while he tasted, sucked, fondled them in turn. The pink, pebbled tips stood at attention, begging for his kiss. But there was more of Diana to explore, and he wanted to please every inch of her.

He trailed her body with his hands and with his lips. Her neck, the inside of her arms, the curve of her hips, the warm flesh of her thighs. His own needs were thundering inside him, but he didn't want them satisfied, didn't want this moment to end.

"Tell me what you want, Diana. Teach me how to please you."

"You don't need any lessons for that." She moaned in pleasure and rubbed her body against his. "Just keep doing what you're doing."

But he wanted perfection. He could never fit into her life on a permanent basis, but he wanted to be the man she thought of when she lay in bed in the middle of the night and felt the urges deep inside her. He wanted her to remember this night the way he knew he always would.

He slipped his fingers beneath her panties. She was already moist, hot to the touch. He couldn't be inside her, not tonight, maybe not ever, but he would make sure she didn't miss a thing.

He kissed her over and over, and she kissed him right back, while his hands roamed her body until she squealed in delight. "I didn't hurt you, did I?"

"Oh, no, you're doing everything right. Perfect." She turned to face him. "You're a hard act to follow, but I'll try."

"You won't have to try long. I'm easy. At least I will be tonight."

She kissed him hard on the mouth, and then she roamed his body, touching him in ways he'd never been touched. Sensual. Teasing. Wanton. Her lips seared into his flesh as she nibbled her way down his stomach, her fingers a fiery blaze when she wrapped them around the length of him.

"Oh, Diana. Diana. Diana." He whispered her name over and over as she stroked him, his body riding a crest of passion that engulfed him so totally, he lost all control. She took him higher and higher until he came in a blast of delirium that took him over the top and then dropped him back to earth, drained of every ounce of energy. He lay beside her, holding her in his arms until his heart slowed to near normal.

There were a lot of things he wanted to say to her, but they'd sound hokey. He wouldn't even tell her he was falling in love with her. It would only complicate things for her. Their lives were too different, their worlds too far apart to ever coexist.

She wrapped her legs around him and rubbed her body against his. "I like the feel of you," she said. "You're all angles and knots and muscle."

"And you're all soft, like a new puppy."

"We make a good team." She ran her big toe up and down his calf. "When this is over—"

He put a finger to her mouth and stopped her sentence. When this was over it would be over, but he didn't want to chill the warmth they'd created tonight with truth. "We have tonight, Diana. All night. Let's not say or do anything to spoil that."

"If that's the way you want it."

But she moved her legs from around him and started to get up. That's when he saw what had to be the tattoo she'd talked about—a tiny series of red dots in the small of her back. He pulled her back for a closer look. "So, biker lady, exactly what is that supposed to be?"

"A heart." She grimaced. "Don't laugh. I told you my toughness was just an illusion. I chickened out before the tattoo artist finished. He was very irritated that I messed up his creation."

Ross watched as she threw her legs over the side of the bed and marched across the room, her behind moving in an easy sway, the red dots shifting and dancing as she went. He didn't know why the artist had complained. He was sure it was the sexiest tattoo he'd ever seen.

She picked up the phone book and flipped to the yellow pages. "I'm famished. Do you think it's safe to order a pizza?"

"Sure. Go ahead."

He walked over and nuzzled her neck while she ordered a large with everything on it. "It will be forty minutes," she said as she hung up the phone.

"That should be just about right." He swooped her up in his arms and carried her back to bed. When the

memories had to last a lifetime, you needed all the re-
inforcement you could get.

DIANA SAT UP IN BED, still braless, but with the rumpled
sheet pulled high enough to cover her legs and the most
intimate body part. "You can set the pizza right here,"
she said, patting a spot in the middle of the bed.

Ross smiled and padded across the floor in his bare
feet. "A motel picnic," he said. "There's nothing like
them."

A weed of jealousy tumbled through her mind.
"Does that bring back memories?"

"It will now." He held up a slice of pizza, the cheese
all gooey and stringing from the box to his hand. He
leaned over and held it for her to sample.

She chewed it, swallowed and smacked her lips. "Either I'm really hungry or that's the best pizza I've ever
eaten."

He climbed back into bed, settling the box between
them. "You should be hungry. You haven't eaten since
breakfast."

Strange, she'd forgotten for a while that she'd missed
lunch. Ross had stopped at a café/gas station combo en
route from their first devastating stop to their second,
but she'd only had coffee. Her stomach had been churning so hard by then that food was the last thing on her
mind.

The events of the day stole their way back into her
mind. She'd begun with high hopes only to have them
crushed and ground into desperation after following up
on the two leads Ross had gotten from his friend.

She couldn't help but wonder if she was setting herself up for the same type of defeat again. The ad in the

newspaper might fall even flatter, but still she had to give it a try.

She took another bite of pizza, but it didn't taste nearly as good as the first bite had. Reality was so cruel. No matter how wonderful it had felt making love with Ross, she could only stay in that state of euphoria for minutes before the truth of their predicament came crashing back down on top of her.

Still, she wasn't sorry they'd made love. She would never be sorry for that.

She half expected Ross to ask her why she'd grown so quiet, but when she turned to look at him, it was evident he'd turned inside himself as well. Wanted for murder, and now, somehow, the police had found out that he was with her. Why else would her home have been surrounded by squad cars and policemen when they'd returned home tonight? From respectable pregnant daughter of the governor of Texas to a woman guilty of aiding and abetting a wanted man.

She felt as if she'd been picked up and sat down in the twilight zone or in some weird horror movie where the plot grew more and more dark and twisted with every scene. A movie where there was no way out.

"Do you mind if I turn on the TV?" Ross asked. "I'd like to catch the evening news."

"Go ahead. We're probably the lead story."

He flicked on the set just as the commercial faded to the anchorwoman sitting straight and tall in front of her fake backdrop.

"Fueled by the recent attack on his life, Governor Thomas Kincaid has vowed anew that he will do everything in his power to put an end to organized crime in Texas during his term in office. Though no charges have been filed in the bomb-planting incident inside the governor's office in Austin, speculation is high that the Mafia is responsible. J. B. Crowe, the frequently reputed head of the crime organization, offered no comment when asked if he claimed responsibility for the attempt on the governor's life.''

"Looks as if your dad is not backing down," Ross said.

"I told you he's a very hardheaded man."

He reached over the pizza and trailed a finger down her arm. "I recognize the family trait."

"Actually, this goes even deeper than just his usual determination. The battle lines between J. B. Crowe and my father were drawn long ago and have been set in stone ever since."

"What happened?"

"They were— Wait, they're talking about you."

The anchorwoman continued, "Ross Taylor, an itinerant cowboy and ex-Dallas police officer arrested last week in the murder of Halpern rancher Darrell Arnold, is still missing and considered dangerous. Police followed up on an anonymous tip today that placed Taylor in the Dallas area, but they now believe that it was a bogus sighting. They warn that Taylor could be anywhere. Police are asking that if you see him or think that you see him, you should call the number on your screen at once. Do not try to apprehend him yourself."

The phone number of the Dallas Police Department and the pencil likeness of Ross flashed on the screen. Ross flicked off the set and hurled the remote control to the end of the bed.

"And there you have it. You are sleeping with a dangerous man."

She moved the pizza box from between them and scooted back into his arms, a means of reassurance, as much for herself as for him. "We're lucky the pizza delivery man didn't recognize you."

"From that picture? Not likely. Besides, I only opened the door a crack when he knocked and then stepped behind it altogether when I handed him the money and took the pizza. I'm sure he thought I had a naked woman in here with me waiting for food."

"You did, at least nearly naked."

"And I still do." He touched his lips to hers.

She kissed him quickly, then pulled away. "I'm worried, Ross. Do you really think that all of those police cars we saw at my house were the result of an anonymous tip?"

"I never fully believe anything I hear on the news. But, I have to admit, I'm surprised they didn't use your name in the report. I expected them to tie the two of us together."

"Maybe since they didn't find you and the tip involved a high-profile politician's daughter, they actually did assume it was just some guy looking for a little fun."

"More likely, they just want me to believe that they're not looking for me around your place so that I'll go back there."

"I never even thought of that." The room grew stuffy, seemed to be closing in around her. One complication after another, all sharp and pointed, pricking and drawing blood.

Ross ran his fingers through her hair, toying with the ends of it. "I told you from the beginning that I was not the man you wanted to invite into your life, Diana. Nothing's changed."

"If I had it to do all over again, I'd still beg you to come with me."

"I can't imagine why?"

"You kept me from panicking while a poisonous snake crawled over my shoe. You saved me from Conan. You got me out of the woods and back to civilization. You've kept me sane. And you just took me to heaven and back—twice. How's that for starters?"

"Maybe I should hire you as my lawyer."

"You'll have the best money can buy, just like I promised, and I can always be a character witness."

"Oh, yeah. The jury will love that part about taking you to heaven and back."

She put her hand on top of his, locking their fingers together. "No jury will convict you, Ross. There's no motive for the killing."

"The state's attorney might not see it quite like you do."

"But you were hit on the head and blacked out. You don't even know who hit you, so why would you wake up and shoot a man you barely knew?"

"I had a reason to quarrel with Darrell Arnold."

"But you said—"

"It was what I didn't say that confused you. The truth is I'd worked two weeks for him. When it was time for him to pay me, he came up with some ridiculous flap about how I'd let one of his calves that had been born prematurely die. He docked me a week's pay. I had gone to the bar that night to collect."

"Why didn't you tell me that when we first talked about it?"

"You were half afraid of me and you'd already been through so much. Looking back, I should have leveled with you from the start, but then I just wanted to ease your mind. Thinking I could be a killer would have terrified you more."

He was right. A week ago, she'd have believed the worst about him. Now she was so under his spell, she'd never believe him capable of doing anything criminal. But what if she was wrong?

Ross hugged her to him, as if he sensed her foreboding. "You didn't finish telling me about your father and J. B. Crowe. What happened to make them such fierce enemies?"

"I only know my dad's side of the story, so it's no doubt slanted. He only sees things in black and white."

"That would make decision-making easy."

"It definitely limits choices. Anyway J.B. and my dad grew up in the same neighborhood, a far cry from the exclusive ones they live in now. According to my dad, J.B. was crooked from the day he was born, but my dad's younger brother Billy didn't see him that way. J.B. and Billy were best friends, and, according to my dad, J.B. led him astray."

"Are Crowe and Billy still friends?"

"Billy was killed before his twentieth birthday, shot in the head during a shoot-out at a convenience store robbery. Supposedly he held the gun, but Dad's convinced that Crowe put him up to it."

"Knowing Crowe like I do, I'd be inclined to agree with your dad."

"At any rate, there's hardly been a civil word exchanged between them since. But I know Crowe has a daughter, and I keep wondering how she feels about having a father who's head of the mob."

"The only good thing I've ever heard about J. B. Crowe is that he's a family man. It's other people's families he tears apart without a shred of conscience."

Diana wrestled with the conflict in her mind. "Two men. Same neighborhood, but one grows up to head an organized crime syndicate. The other grows up to be the governor of Texas. It makes you wonder what really makes a man who and what he is.''

''If you find the answer to that, you'll have the Pulitzer in the palm of your hand.''

But it wasn't the Pulitzer she wanted in her hand. What she wanted was Alexandra in her arms. She lay back on the pillow, images of her baby playing in her mind. She fell asleep planning the ad she'd place in the morning.

Wanted: A woman so desperate for a baby of her own that she'd consider playing games with a madman. The wording would be different. The meaning would be the same.

Diana would be playing with the same madman.

# Chapter Fourteen

Ross flicked off the television set, tired of channel surfing when his mind was too beleaguered with problems to concentrate on anything Saturday afternoon had to offer. It was their second day in the motel, and as much as he enjoyed being with Diana, the endless waiting was driving him nuts. He'd made another phone call to the Garrett ranch and Finders Keepers yesterday. Lily had said Dylan wasn't in and wouldn't be back anytime soon, but she'd give him the message if he called home.

Ross settled back in the uncomfortable chair and his gaze settled on Diana, her head bent over a tablet she'd purchased that morning, a yellow pencil idle between her fingers. A twinge of desire sidled through him.

Two people caught in a desperate situation. Diana frantically searching for her child. He, an ex-cop who'd once wanted nothing more than to fight crime, now one of the most wanted fugitives in Texas. Both of them with nerves frazzled to the point of breaking, with emotions raging as wildly as the newest roller coaster at Six Flags Over Texas.

And yet he'd never felt this way about a woman before, never wanted to imagine what it would be like to wake up next to her every morning for the rest of his life. And now that he did, the relationship had nowhere to go.

Diana was the governor's daughter, a *very* rich governor's daughter. He was an itinerant cowboy with a lengthy murder trial and maybe a jail sentence to face. Possibly more than a jail sentence if he was found guilty of murdering Darrell Arnold, but he refused to think of that now. He had his hands full just trying to keep Diana safe.

He was sure J. B. Crowe was the mastermind behind her abduction and the theft of her baby. The timing was too perfect, coming at a point when the situation between Crowe and the governor was quickly escalating into a full-scale war.

Besides, the kidnapping and baby theft were exactly the kind of things Crowe would dream up, the ultimate way to teach Thomas Kincaid a lesson. Sick, cruel, totally heartless. And Ross knew all too well that once Crowe made up his mind to do something, he wouldn't let a simple thing like Diana's escape stand in his way. But this time Crowe *would not win.*

He stood, walked over and fit his hands about her shoulders, massaging her tense muscles. She lay down her pencil and picked up the tablet. "Will you take a look at these questions for me? I don't want to scare the respondents off, but I need to know if they've ever been contacted by someone offering to sell them a baby, or contacted by someone saying anything that made them think the people were working outside the legal realms of adoption."

He took the paper from her and skimmed the interview form. The questions were direct and intrusive, but she'd cloaked them in professional terminology, and a woman desperate to obtain a child probably wouldn't hesitate to answer them.

"They look fine to me."

She bit her bottom lip. "I have to keep it concise, make it sound like a typical preliminary phone interview, but still do the job."

"It's definitely to the point. I don't know enough about adoptions to know if it's typical."

"I'm not sure, either. I wish I had access to my computer so I could check the Internet for information, but this will have to do. If it appears they might have had contact with someone from the black-market baby ring, I'll have to convince them to set up an interview with me."

"All that will take time."

"Not if it works according to plan. I'll tell them I'm only in town for two days, that my agency works out of New Orleans. That way they'll know they have to see me at once if they're interested. And somehow I'll make sure they're interested."

"Sounds as if you have it all figured out."

"I know it seems crazy to you, but it could work, and I have nothing to lose. If they'll talk to me in person, I'll tell them what happened to me and beg them to give me the name and contact information so that I can track down my baby. Any woman will be able to understand my anguish. How could they not help me? If I can connect with the right person."

And that was the rub. It was just an ad in the paper, and he couldn't imagine it would give her the results she was looking for. A sixth of a page, eye-catching layout, appropriate for the type of service she was advertising. At least that's what the salesman had promised when she'd said she wanted it to run Sunday and didn't have time to provide the copy layout herself.

He glanced at his watch. It should hit the newsstand approximately fifteen hours from now. If there were no calls to Diana's cellular phone tomorrow, or if the calls didn't provide her with the information she needed, she'd be devastated.

In the meantime, there was nothing to do but wait. He'd never felt more useless. Not to mention that he was suffering from a severe case of cabin fever.

They'd slipped out of the motel for a while that morning, long enough to go to the drugstore around the corner. They'd picked up a few essentials, toothbrushes, toothpaste, razors, the tablet, that sort of thing. He'd also purchased a pair of sunglasses to make it a little more difficult to identify him.

He could have planned a full disguise, but time was running out. Diana could only fool her parents for a few more days at the most. After that, the theft of her baby would be out in the open and he would be forced to turn himself in and leave Diana's protection to someone else.

The cellular phone rang. Diana jumped at the sound and choked on the sip of coffee she'd been about to swallow. It splattered from her lips and painted the front of the white blouse she was wearing with runners of brown stain.

She answered the phone and then handed it to him. "It's Dylan Garrett." Leaving him to his conversation, she headed for the bathroom to try to wash out the spills before the stains set.

He turned away, thinking it might be best if she didn't hear all of this conversation. "I was hoping you'd return my call," Ross said.

"Lily gave me the message when I called home. What's up?"

"Not a lot, but I thought I'd bring you up-to-date. We visited the two people Lily suggested. We got exactly nowhere, but I have a couple of other questions you might be able to answer."

There was a pause. It lasted so long Ross thought they might have lost their connection until he heard Dylan clear his throat.

"Why didn't you level with me, Ross?"

"I told you what I could."

"You didn't tell me that the woman you were trying to help was Diana Kincaid."

"How did you find out?"

"I'm a math whiz, remember. I put two and two together. And so has Zach Logan."

"I thought you'd retired from police work."

"I have. To paraphrase a quote, these are the times that try men's souls and make Zach Logan very nervous."

"So he called you back into the game."

"You didn't hear that from me."

"So Zach knows everything. I guess that explains the horde of cops who descended on her house last night."

"If you'd been there, you'd have been arrested."

"Or if I showed up anytime thereafter. So much for the anonymous tip. I guess Zach Logan released that information to the media as well."

"Zach did what he had to, but I don't know why you're complaining. At least in jail, you'd have a halfway decent chance of staying alive. Now how about giving me the full story?"

Ross filled him in on the details of Diana's abduction and of her baby being supposedly sold on the black market. Dylan knew too much for them to try to keep the rest a secret and he just might be able to help them.

"If Crowe hasn't figured out that you're the cowboy in question, he will soon enough. When he does, he'll come after you, and he won't be looking to drive you to jail."

"I'm sure he's figured it all out by now," Ross said. "Not only did I escape near the area where Diana was rescued, but one of his flunkies got a good look at me when I clubbed him and kicked the pistol out of his hand."

"So Crowe did kidnap the governor's daughter. Zach had the feeling something big was up. He just didn't know how big. When Kincaid finds out Crowe not only kidnapped his daughter but stole his granddaughter, this is going to blow sky-high."

"So much for the good news."

"Zach wants you to turn yourself in, Ross. He'll take over the case and Diana's protection."

"He provided protection for my brother. He's dead. And Zach's been working on getting Crowe for years, and he's still walking around a free man. Tell him thanks for the offer, but I think Diana and I will keep doing this our way, at least for a few more days."

"So the two of you are just going to keep looking for the baby on your own?"

"It's the way she wants it, and it's her baby."

He could hear Dylan's sigh of exasperation over the phone. When he spoke again his voice had acquired a dead serious edge. "I told Zach you'd see it that way. I don't blame you. I'd probably see it that way myself if I were standing in your shoes. But walk careful, old pal. Watch your back. And write down this number. It's my pager. Just in case you need backup."

Ross committed the number to memory as Dylan rattled it off and then broke the connection. He hadn't asked his questions, but Dylan had answered them anyway. The police knew he was with Diana. And he was sure Crowe did as well.

And J. B. Crowe hated Ross Taylor almost as much as he hated Governor Kincaid. Maybe more.

DIANA ROLLED OVER in bed so that she could see the illuminated dial of the clock. It was 2:00 a.m. She slid from beneath the covers, quietly, so as not to wake Ross. But he stirred and reached for her.

"You need to get some sleep, Diana."

"I know, but I can't. I keep thinking about Alexandra. It's like my heart's outside of me. I keep reaching for it, but it's not there."

"A mother's love. They say there's nothing like it." He tugged her back beside him.

"I'm beginning to understand what it must have been like for my mother when I went through my rebellious stage. She was always caught in the middle between Dad and me, loving the both of us."

"I'm sure your father loved you, too. Men may show emotions differently, but we do have them. We just hide them better, carry them around inside us while we play tough so that women don't notice."

"I know he loved me. He still does. I've thought about what you said about our being alike, both of us wanting to do things our way. I inherited his stubbornness and it reached its peak when I was an adolescent. Unfortunately it carried over into my college years and even when I started med school. I felt I had to prove myself—on my terms."

"I think they call that growing up."

"I guess."

"At least you grew out of your rebellious stage in time to get your life together. My brother didn't. By the time he realized the error of his ways, it was too late. Thanks to J. B. Crowe."

The bitterness crept into his voice and tensed his muscles, the way it always did when Crowe came into the conversation. She snuggled against him, amazed that in the midst of all she was going through, she could feel so deeply for this rugged cowboy she knew so little about. Twinges of guilt over being with anyone who wasn't Alex still hit occasionally, but not with the force they'd first carried. Alex Hastings would be the last person to expect her never to love again.

Ross stroked her arms, soothing her, trying to lull her back to sleep. She closed her eyes, but sleep didn't come. Instead her mind flooded with the images of the baby she'd held in her arms those few brief moments.

*Mommy loves you, Alexandra. And I'm coming to get you. One day soon.*

## DAY 10

ROSS NURSED a cup of strong, black coffee and studied the ad. It was eye-catching, just as the salesman from the paper had promised. A picture of a baby wrapped in a blanket directly in the center with the message arranged around it in large, bold print.

Do you long to have a baby of your own but have been turned down for adoption by traditional agencies? Can you provide love, nurturing and a good home, but can't meet one of the other requirements? If so, we may be able to help your dreams come true. Call today for a confidential assessment of your ability to meet our more realistic requirements.

"So much for truth in advertising," he commented, pushing the ad aside. "You may get a lot of angry callers when they find out you can't deliver."

"I know. I thought about that this morning when I read the actual ad. I hate that I'm getting some people's hopes up for nothing, but I have no other choice." She chewed on her bottom lip and ran her finger up and down the edge of the tablet where she'd written out the questions she hadn't had a chance to try.

A few minutes later, the first call of the day came in. He watched her face as she talked, and knew immediately the call was not going well. By the time she hung up the phone, the desperation had already settled into thin lines around her tired eyes and caused her slender shoulders to droop.

"They'd visited two local agencies," Diana said, giving Ross the details of the call. "They're on the waiting list of one, but they don't want to wait. The woman sounded shocked and then suspicious when I asked if anyone had ever contacted her about obtaining a baby without going through all the legal channels. At that point, she decided I wasn't the person to help her fulfill her dreams of adoption."

Diana dropped to the couch beside him. "You were probably right about this being a waste of time."

"I never said it was a waste of time. I said it was a long shot. And it's only nine in the morning. Most people haven't even read the paper yet."

"Now you're just trying to make me feel better."

"And what's wrong with that?" He did hate to see

her disappointed so quickly, but nothing he could do or say was going to make this day any easier.

If he weren't a wanted man, if he were free to be out there and beat down doors, track down his old inform-ers… No, he was only fooling himself.

He'd tried for six months to get something on J. B. Crowe. Hounded people until he'd lost his job. And still he'd gotten nowhere. Neither had Zach Logan and his antimob task force and they'd been at it a lot longer than Ross. But, someday the man would make a mis-take. Ross just hoped he was around to enjoy it when they finally locked him behind bars.

DIANA TOSSED her phone to the bed where Ross was stretched out with his eyes closed. "Okay, I've had it. I don't think I'll take another call."

"What was wrong with this caller? Wait. Don't tell me. Let me guess. We've had an eighty-year-old woman in the nursing home who said she'd been trying for ten years to adopt and they keep telling her she's too old. And a woman in prison who wanted to adopt so she'll have a better chance of having the parole board grant her request for release."

"And don't forget the woman who wanted a baby so that her mother would put her back into the will even though she was living with her mother's ex-husband." Diana kicked off her shoes and joined him on the bed. "I should have known an ad like this would bring out all kinds, but I thought there would be more normal peo-ple who for some reason just didn't qualify as adoptive parents. I was thinking something like an older husband, a woman with health problems, an unmarried woman."

"You got a few of those."

"Too few. And no one who'd ever been contacted

by someone offering to provide a baby for cash, no questions asked, no legal documents.''

''At least no one willing to admit it.''

''But there is a black-market baby ring,'' she insisted. ''So someone out there has to know something. Maybe that's what I should have put in the ad. If you've ever bought or sold a baby, give me a call.''

''You'd have gotten dozens. All people wanting to get on your daytime TV show.''

The phone rang again, and in spite of her vow not to answer it, she lunged for the phone.

DIANA TOOK a deep breath and punched the talk button. ''Good evening, are you calling about our ad in today's paper?''

''Diana, is that you?''

''Oh, hi, Mom. Yeah it's me, just a private joke. I thought you'd be someone else calling.''

''Are you sure you're all right?''

''Couldn't be better.'' The lie was so ridiculous it didn't even register on her guilt scale.

''Where are you? I tried your home phone, but you didn't answer.''

''It's out of order. I'm relying on my cellular phone this weekend.''

''You need to get the telephone company out there the first thing in the morning. It's not a good time to be without service. You could go into labor any minute now. You haven't, have you?''

Diana clutched the phone a little tighter. There was no use to go on with the masquerade. No use to try and protect her parents from the truth. She couldn't do it forever. Sooner or later, they'd have to know that Alexandra was missing.

But not tonight. Dear, Lord, not tonight. In spite of the quips she'd exchanged with Ross a few minutes ago, she was dying inside. She'd done all she could do, but she just couldn't deal with telling her mother the whole heartbreaking story tonight.

"Diana, what's wrong. Are you sure you're all right?"

"I'm just tired."

"You're probably not getting enough rest. You need someone to look after you. I've already told your father that I'm flying back to Dallas tomorrow. I can't sit around this governor's mansion another day worrying about your being there by yourself when you go into labor."

"The baby's not due for a few days, and first babies are usually late."

"That doesn't mean a thing. You were two weeks early. I didn't even have the nursery finished when I had to rush to the hospital."

She finished the conversation with her mom and then glanced at the clock. Ten minutes before four. No one would be calling about an adoption this late. Every road she'd tried had been a dead end. Now her mother was coming home. She'd find out that Diana was no longer pregnant and that her baby was missing. The search would be out of her hands.

The battle would be between her father and J. B. Crowe. It would go on and on and on, the way it always had. Everyone would claim to be looking for Alexandra, only they'd really be tied up in their own anger and resentment, their own need for revenge.

It was over.

She should be crying, shaking her fists in rage, or screaming at the top of her lungs. Instead she felt—empty. So empty that she hardly felt at all.

"I give up, Ross."

He took her in his arms and held her close, gently as if he realized she had no heart left inside her. "What are you talking about? Did your mother say something to upset you?"

"She's coming home tomorrow. She wants to be here when I go into labor."

"What will you do?"

"Tell her the truth. We'll call my dad and call the police, maybe even the FBI. I'll have to trust them to find my daughter."

"And they will, Diana."

"Sure. How many kids go missing every year and are never heard from again? And they're not taken by people nearly as talented at what they do as the Texas mafia."

"This is different. Your father's the governor. The case will be top priority."

"The case will be a media circus. Eventually, after everyone throws around enough blame, someone may find her. In the meantime, all I can do is pray that she's safe." She sighed and nestled close to his heart. "What about you, Ross? What will you do?"

"Turn myself in."

"I meant what I said. I'll stand behind you, get you the best lawyer money can buy. You'll be free—"

The phone rang again. She hated to answer it, but she knew she would. "Hello."

"I'm calling about the ad that was in the paper today."

It was the first male caller she'd had all day, and the minute he spoke, she had the strange feeling that she'd just hit pay dirt.

# Chapter Fifteen

Diana pressed the phone against her ear. "Can you speak up? I can barely hear you."

"I don't want my wife to know I'm calling you. We're staying at the Holiday Inn and she's in the bathroom so I have to make this quick."

"How can I help you?"

"You said the call would be confidential?"

"That's correct."

"So I don't have to give you my name?"

"Not if you don't want to at this time." She'd have to treat this man with kid gloves. He was a nervous wreck, and it wouldn't take much for him to panic and hang up on her.

"I read your ad, and we definitely fit the profile you're looking for. We've been turned down by every agency in Texas."

"Why is that?"

"My wife has some problems."

"Health problems?"

"Right, with her nerves, you know. She's all right some days but other days she just can't cope. Cries, throws tantrums, occasionally tries to kill herself. The shrink calls it a personality disorder, not that she's crazy or anything. He put her on a new medicine, and she's a lot better now.''

Diana ignored the questions on her list. She had to sound sympathetic, win his confidence. ''Modern medicines are certainly a miracle. Are you still interested in adoption?''

''Actually, we're already getting a baby. That's why we're in town. We drove over from Kilgore. I'm just a little concerned about the way it's being handled.''

''Is this a legal adoption?''

''The man who's arranging it claims it is. They're going to give us some kind of paper when we give them the money. But I haven't signed anything, and they're insisting the payment be one lump sum in cash.''

The excitement surged inside her, and she had to work to keep her voice steady. ''What is the money for?''

''The biological mother's medical bills, court costs, lawyer's fees. I don't know. There's a whole list of expenses, but fifty thousand dollars seems exorbitant to me. It's our whole life's savings up to this point. It's worth it, I guess, to get a baby. At least it's worth it to my wife, but I hate to be played for a sucker.''

Diana reached for the pencil and tablet, her hands shaking so badly, she could barely pick them up. ''I need to talk to you in person.''

''I can't do that. My wife would be furious if she knew I was even talking to you about this on the phone. I don't expect you to do anything. I just wanted to know what you thought about this kind of deal.''

''I think you're being taken, and please don't hang up. I can help you.''

''I wish I'd called you sooner. It's really too late now. We're all set to pick up the baby first thing in the morning. And the people running the operation have stressed that we shouldn't talk to anyone about this.''

"That should tell you that something's wrong."

"They said the state didn't sanction these adoptions but they assured us that they're federally approved.''

Her mind whirled, sure she was finally on to something, determined to find an argument that would get through to this man. "I don't believe them. I think this is an illegal adoption and you are likely to lose the money and still have to give up the baby at some point. Please, for your wife's sake as well as yours, let me come to the motel and talk to you.''

"No, I can't upset my wife. She's—fragile. You understand. I don't know why I called. We're on a runaway horse and there's no stopping it now."

"Where are you picking up the baby?"

"I gotta go. I hear the toilet flushing."

"No, just tell me when and where—" She was still talking when the connection went dead. She scribbled down the man's phone number.

She didn't realize Ross was at her elbow until the phone conversation had ended. Evidently the urgency in her voice had captured his attention.

"Did you learn something that will help?"

"I'm not sure." Her heart seemed to have jumped to her throat, but still it was racing like crazy. "I have a phone number, and a couple who are exchanging fifty thousand dollars for a baby tomorrow morning."

Shock registered on Ross's face. "Son of a gun! You just may have struck oil. Give me the facts."

"I don't have many. It was the husband who called. He refused to give his name, but he did say that he and his wife are staying at a Holiday Inn. He didn't say which one."

"We're lucky he gave you the phone number."

"He didn't. My phone has a caller ID function." She handed him the tablet. "If you can find which Holiday Inn the couple's staying at and get me a room number to go with it, I think we're in business."

ROSS THANKED DYLAN for his investigative work, tossed the phone to the bed and swooped Diana into his arms. He whirled her around the room until he was so dizzy he collapsed on the bed, still holding her in his arms.

"Does that mean Dylan Garrett was able to track down the motel?"

"Oh, baby, he and Zach Logan got a lot more than that. Mr. and Mrs. Dwayne Bolin are staying in room 206 of the Holiday Inn on the LBJ Freeway, out in Garland. Their 1996 Ford van, with an infant seat already strapped into place, is parked in the north parking lot."

Diana's beautiful green eyes grew wide, and her face lit up like New Year's Eve. "You're kidding."

"Total truth." He slapped his right hand over his heart. "Scout's honor."

She squealed and jumped a foot off the floor, twirling around the room before she stopped and threw her arms around him. "But how could they get all of that from one phone number?"

"It's what detectives do. They got the specific Holiday Inn and room number from the phone number you gave me. The name of the couple came from the clerk on duty and the rest is all a matter of record. Except for the spot where the van is parked. Zach had one of his officers on duty in that area check that out."

"That's amazing."

"No, Diana. *You* are amazing. You're the one who made this happen." He kissed her hard on the mouth, drunk on relief and excitement and most of all on Diana.

She kissed him back, wild yet sweet, and he hated it to end, but there was so much to talk about, not all of it good. "I hate to always be the pessimist, but you need to remember that there is no guarantee that this actually involves the men from the black-market smuggling ring or that they are associated with the men who took your daughter."

"I realize there are no guarantees, but I really think this is the lead we've been looking for. Dylan must think so, too."

"He's hopeful. So is Zach Logan."

"How did he get in on this?"

"Dylan had to tell him what was going on. We need his help. He has cops staking out the van now, but Zach and Dylan are going to take over the 4:00 a.m. shift. They'll follow the car and if the baby exchange takes place, they'll make an arrest. They've very reluctantly agreed that I can go with them, under watchful eye of a police officer."

"Of course, *we'll* be there."

He knew that was coming, but he also knew Zach would never take the governor's daughter into an explosive situation like this. "I'm sorry, honey, but if these are the men we're looking for, there's no telling how they'll react when they realize the deal has gone bad. There could be gunplay and both Zach and Dylan made it clear, this is no place for a civilian."

"No place for a civilian." Her voice rose, her hands flew to her hips and her eyes flashed fire. "I've been kidnapped, had my baby delivered by some quack and then ripped from my arms. I've tramped through the woods with killers chasing me and slept in a shack with scorpions. I have earned my spot on the arrest team, and I *am* going to be there in the morning when these baby marketeers are arrested. With or without you and this Zach Logan and Dylan Garrett you keep talking about.''

He put up his hands as if to ward off the tirade, but he couldn't wipe the smile from his face. Diana Kincaid was one hell of a woman. ''I tell you what. You explain all of that to Zach Logan. I'd like to see him tell you no.''

''I'd like to see him try.'' She climbed onto his lap, and a crazy streak of desire shot through him. As ridiculous as it seemed, he was going to miss being on the run with Diana Kincaid.

''Remember that if this doesn't work out the way you hope it does, it doesn't mean all is lost,'' he reminded her. ''You'll still be working with Dylan and Zach Logan to find Alexandra.''

''I can't think like that. I have to believe that this will lead to my getting my daughter back.''

He'd said his piece, and he wasn't going to argue with her tonight.

''You know, Ross, it speaks well of your past experiences on the Dallas Police Force that Zach Logan is taking you along tomorrow when you're still officially wanted for murder.''

''That's because the men with the baby won't be the only ones taken into custody. I'll go to the scene of the exchange, but I'll be considered in custody. After that, I'll return to the station house with Zach. Thankfully he's going to let me turn myself in, rather than drag me along in handcuffs.''

''So this is your last night of freedom.''

He took her hands in his and touched them to his lips. "This is it."

The fire had gone out of her eyes. Now they were shadowed, haunted.

"I'll be fine, Diana. I know this very rich, smart and sexy lady who's promised to get me the best lawyer money can buy. She also told me that if I'm innocent I'll have nothing to fear."

"It's not you I'm worried about," she quipped, and they both knew she was lying. "It's me, and what I'll do without you."

"You're tough. You'll do just fine." The truth of his statement grated along the edges of his heart. When this was over she wouldn't need him. But how was he ever going to stop needing her?

She wrapped her arms around his neck. "Make love with me, Ross. It may have to last a while, so make it good."

"Have I ever made it any other way?" he teased, trying desperately to keep the moment upbeat.

"Never."

And he didn't plan for tonight to be the exception. It would probably have to last forever.

## DAY 11

DIANA STRETCHED her legs, already tired of sitting and waiting, but she wouldn't have missed this for anything. The Bolins were going to pick up a baby, and even though she was afraid to even think it, she prayed that baby would be Alexandra.

Ross was in the driver's seat next to her and a cop appointed by Zach Logan was in the back seat so that he could keep a watchful eye on Ross at all times.

"This is it," Ross said, sitting up straight. "Mr. Bolin, I presume. And just in time for the morning traffic jam."

She watched as a man who looked to be in his mid-fifties walked up to the back of the van, a duffel bag slung over each shoulder.

The man opened the hatch and pitched one of the small pieces of mismatched luggage inside. By the time he finished, a woman was hurrying toward him. She appeared to be younger than him, maybe forty-five or so, and so thin she could have posed for an ad depicting the perils of starvation. Still, she was attractive in a girlish sort of way. Her hair was long and straight and she wore almost no makeup, though her lips were tinted a soft pink.

A woman with problems, at least according to her husband, but Diana could identify with her desire for a baby to hold in her arms. Mr. Bolin opened the door for his wife, and she climbed into the van on the passenger side. Her full skirt hung low and she yanked it up to keep it from getting caught in the door. Mr. Bolin closed it for her, then deposited the other piece of luggage onto the seat behind her.

He was dressed in jeans, well-worn but clean, and a starched white shirt that he'd left open at the neck. His boots were functional and scuffed and the western hat showed signs of sun and rain.

Ross fit Diana's key into the ignition of her BMW. "They don't look like the type of people who can afford to drop fifty thousand dollars."

"I was thinking the same thing," Diana said. "It makes me sad and even angrier to realize the kind of people the men who run this operation are preying on."

"I know. We kept thinking they'd go to people who

could afford to pay, but obviously that's not the case. They just look for the ones who are either desperate or gullible enough to fall for their scheme.''

"And some of the people who fall into that category are grossly unfit for parenthood, like Mrs. Bolin with all her emotional problems. The legitimate adoption agencies screened her out, and the baby ring stepped in.''

They were talking as if this were a done deal, as if they knew for a fact the Bolin adoption had been orchestrated by the black-market operation. But as much as Diana hated to admit it, she knew they couldn't be certain. Still, fifty thousand dollars and no legal work were strong indicators they were right.

The taillights of the van glowed red as Mr. Bolin backed from his parking space. Zach Logan and Dylan Garrett would follow the van. Ross and Diana and the police officer in the back seat would follow them a few cars behind to avoid detection, but close enough to keep the van in sight at all times.

Zach had staunchly refused to allow her to come along when she'd first approached him with the idea. She'd told him the only way he could keep her away was to lock her in jail, and for a minute, she thought he would. But, in the end, he'd relented, though he'd made her promise she would not get in the way of the sting.

The van bounced over a speed bump on its way to the parking lot exit. As soon as it turned onto the road in front of the motel, Zach pulled out of his space and followed. A second later the engine in her car purred to life and the three of them were on their way.

The van pulled onto the LBJ Freeway, heading west. As Ross had predicted, the traffic was heavy. Zach had considered using a police helicopter to help keep the van in view, but Ross had persuaded him not to. The last thing they wanted was to alert the men with the baby that something was up.

They passed Central Express Way and kept going. The van pulled into the far left lane.

"Doesn't look as if he's considering exiting anytime soon," the cop commented.

"They'll have to," she insisted. "Surely they wouldn't have stopped in Dallas to spend the night unless this is where the exchange is going to take place."

"The exchange. Their money for someone's baby. I wonder whose this time."

"I'm praying it's mine."

"Anything's possible," Ross reminded her. "You proved that yesterday when you took the call from Mr. Bolin." He reached across and squeezed her hand. "Just don't count on it too much."

"Try telling that to my heart."

Traffic slowed and a truck pulled in between the BMW and the car in front of them. For a few seconds, she lost sight of the van and Zach's vehicle. Panic swelled inside her, and she scooted around in her seat, stretching, frantic for a glimpse of the van.

A moment later, Ross switched lanes, and the van was there, a few cars ahead, still in the far left lane. But the panic didn't subside. That brief moment had seemed like a preview of all that could go wrong.

"Not much left out this way except the airport," Ross said. And as if the driver of the van had heard him, he changed to the center lane, but kept his right-turn blinker on.

The airport. Love Field. Now Diana knew why the

panic had persisted. "If they're catching a flight to another city, we may lose them completely."

"We don't know that they are."

But she heard the strain in his voice and knew he feared the same thing. She leaned back, silent, unmoving while she regrouped. The airport would make it more difficult, but not impossible. If the Bolins flew out, then they could, too. If not all of them, then at least Zach Logan and Dylan Garrett.

The van swerved into the exit lane for Love Field. Zach followed, leaving only two cars between him and the van now. Ross pulled in right behind Zach as he slowed to a safe exit speed.

Once off the freeway, they headed south, bringing them ever closer to the airport entrance. "We'll follow them into the parking area," Ross said. "If it looks like there's no place to park near them, we'll move past them, then turn and double back."

The cop in the back seat didn't protest, but the Bolins didn't move into the lane for airport parking. They followed the signs to passenger pickup. Tailing them became more difficult. Cars pulled in and out of the slow-moving line of traffic as people stopped to pick up waiting passengers and load their luggage. Policemen blew whistles, trying to keep the middle lanes open, moving people along when there was no room to stop.

The van appeared to be just driving through, leading them on a wild-goose chase through the bustling airport. Did they know they were being followed? Were the men with the baby behind them somewhere, watching them and telling them what to do? Had she misunderstood what Dwayne Bolin had said last night about picking up the baby this morning or had he been mistaken about the plans?

The questions rattled around in her brain. The van swerved to the left, into a spot just vacated by an SUV. Zach was following too close to stop without blocking traffic and causing a scene that would alert the baby thieves. Fortunately, Ross and she were several cars behind. He slowed the BMW, inching along as if he were looking for someone. A car pulled out in front of him and he zipped into the spot it had vacated.

Diana breathed a little easier. She could see the van clearly now, and neither Mr. nor Mrs. Bolin were making a move to get out of the vehicle.

"They can't stay parked there long," Ross said. "So we just wait and watch."

They didn't have to wait long. A man and a woman exited the automatic doors, carrying a small piece of luggage—and a baby. Diana's heart slammed against her chest, as the man turned to face them. "That's him, Ross. That's Conan."

"Bingo." Ross opened the car door as Conan and the woman with the baby crawled into the back seat of the van. "I know you don't have to do it," Ross said to the cop in the back seat, "but I'm going to ask you to stay in the car until I signal you to join me. I'll be right here in plain sight, but if they see a uniformed cop, it could blow the whole thing."

"Dylan said I could trust you. Go for it, but I'll be right here watching your every move."

Diana grabbed his arm. "You're not supposed to do this by yourself. Where's Zach?"

"Up ahead. It's all under control. Almost over. Just stay put."

She let go of his arm and watched him walk to the van, shoulders back, a brisk pace, never looking to the right or to the left. A cowboy with the instincts of a cop. She didn't know how she'd figured that out back in the woods, didn't know how she'd had the good sense to talk a man accused of murder into helping her search for her baby, but it had been the luckiest and wisest decision of her life.

Ross NEARED THE VAN. He'd lied to Diana. He didn't have a clue where Zach and Dylan were, but there was no time to wait. He walked past the van, slowly, glancing inside. Mrs. Bolin was holding the baby now, and Conan was unzipping the luggage that her husband had placed in the back seat. Fifty thousand dollars. Ross was sure of it. The exchange was going down and Zach was nowhere around.

Ross was unarmed, unofficial and at least fifty pounds lighter than the giant he was about to face, but he couldn't risk blowing it by having the uniformed cop jump out and start running toward them. He had to act now, on his own. Fueled by an adrenaline rush, he stepped to the side of the van and swung the passenger-side door open.

"You're under arrest. Keep your hands in the air and get out of the van slowly."

"We haven't done anything," Mrs. Bolin insisted.

"I told you this was a mistake," her husband ranted. "You can't just *buy* a baby."

The woman in the back seat pulled a gun from somewhere and pointed it at Ross's head. Conan held on to the suitcase with both hands. "You're no cop, Ross Taylor. You're a killer, just like your brother was. Only you're running around posing as a hero for Diana Kincaid." He tilted his head toward his female accomplice. "Shoot him."

Sirens sounded. Blue lights flashed. Ross dived to the ground as the crack of gunfire shattered the morning.

DIANA JUMPED from the car and followed the cop, running toward the van, charging through the clumps of people who blocked her path. Promises to stay out of the fray meant nothing now. Ross reached out and grabbed her arm as she neared the van, pulling her close.

"I thought you'd been shot," she cried.

"Not him," Zach answered, fastening handcuffs around Conan's wrists while Dylan did the same for the female accomplice. "The side of that building has a nice little hole in it, though." She stared at the bullet hole in the concrete wall and went weak.

"Diana Kincaid." Conan hurled her name into the air as if it were some filthy curse. "I should have finished you off while you lay there screaming for your dead husband."

She ignored him and stuck her head inside the open door of the van. Mrs. Bolin was wailing and holding the baby against her chest. Diana touched her hand to the back of the baby's head. "May I see her?"

The woman quit wailing and met Diana's gaze. "You're going to take her away, aren't you?"

"I'm sorry, Mrs. Bolin, but babies are too precious to be bought and sold like a loaf of bread." She leaned in closer and tugged the flannel blanket away from the baby's face. Hair as light as summer wheat. Big blue eyes. A puckered chin. The baby was adorable, but not Alexandra.

The pain was tremendous, a raking and clawing into her chest as if some mechanical monster were mutilating her still-racing heart. The fury was worse. She turned on Conan, and began to beat her fists against his chest. "Where is Alexandra? What did you do with her?"

"Get this crazy bitch off of me."

They were surrounded by cops now, but it was Ross who pulled her away, rocking her against him.

Conan glared at her from the few feet that separated them, his eyes as cold and hard as Arctic rock. "I told you back at the cabin, Diana. You will *never* see your baby again."

"I'll drive Diana home for you," Dylan said. "I'll get one of the officers to follow and pick me up."

"Thanks. I'd appreciate that."

"I think we're the ones who owe you the thanks. You always were a good cop. But more than that. You're a good man."

Diana leaned against Ross. Two of the perpetrators of the black-market baby ring had been caught in the act, but the victory was hollow. Crowe was not with them and Alexandra was still missing. And now she wouldn't even have Ross to help in her search. He'd be locked away, awaiting his trial.

She shivered, cold, empty. Even the tears had dried up.

"It's not over, Diana," Zach Logan assured her. "There will be a full investigation. The police will dig through all the information and track down as many of the babies as they can. They'll find your daughter."

"I know. I had just hoped it would happen today."

ROSS OPENED HIS ARMS and she fit herself inside them. He'd never liked goodbyes. He hated this one, hated leaving Diana before she had her daughter back. Hated leaving her to someone else's protection. But he had no choice. He couldn't see her face, but he knew her eyes would be wet with tears.

It took him thirty-six years to find a woman he could love. Too bad he hadn't chosen one he could keep.

DIANA SAW her dad's car parked in front of her house the minute they turned the corner. "My mother," she groaned. "I forgot all about her coming in today. I know she told me she was going to fly, but I'm sure that's Dad's car so she must have decided to drive."

"I'm glad she's here," Dylan said. "I won't feel so bad about leaving you alone now and I can tell Ross I left you in good hands."

"Well, at least one of us is glad. Not that I don't want to see her, but this means I have to explain everything to her. Tell her I gave birth to her granddaughter and admit that I don't have a clue as to where they've taken Alexandra. I'll have her grief to deal with as well as my own, and I'm just not sure I'm up to it."

"You'd have to tell your parents anyway. Breaking up the black-market baby ring is big news. There's no way to keep it out of the newspaper."

"I didn't even think about that." She stretched her arms and legs in front of her, working out the kinks the tension of the morning had knotted into them. "Do you think I'll have to testify?"

"More than likely. About your own kidnapping as well as having your baby stolen. You're the only one who can place Conan in both situations, though I doubt Conan is his real name. People in his line of work almost always use an alias when they're on a job."

"His line of work. You say that like it's a career."

"It is. He does the dirty work so the men in charge can keep their hands clean. Kind of like a factory worker who handles the machinery in a hot warehouse while the president of the company sits in an air-conditioned office in a suit and tie.''

''Only the president of the company doesn't break the law and ruin people's lives.''

''It was just an analogy, probably not a good one.''

''Tell Ross I'll be in to see him later.''

''I'll do that.''

She missed him already as she hurried up the walk to her front door. Missed him so much it hurt, but even if he were here, she'd have to be the one to face her mother with the truth. Alexandra was gone, and no one had a clue how to get her back.

# Chapter Sixteen

Diana sat at the table and watched her parents go through the same hell she'd been through the last week and a half. She told them everything. The facts were better coming from her than through newspaper headlines and television news shows.

It was difficult seeing the hurt in her mother's face, watching the tears fill her eyes and fall to the tabletop. Just as hard to watch the transformation of her father. She'd always seen him as emotionless, the tough family leader, the man who never wavered, never weakened. But he'd shuddered more than once as she'd told of her experiences, and it was as if she could see him age before her eyes.

She'd never doubted that he loved her, in his own way, but she'd never had a clue that the love ran so deep. And she'd never realized until this minute how much they both meant to her.

When the story was over, they dissolved into a three-way hug, each holding on to the others as if they might never let go. Finally her dad pulled away.

"It's my fault," he said. "I let this happen."

"It's not your fault. How could it be?"

"Your mother told me to call in the FBI, the state

troopers, every lawman in Texas, but I insisted on conducting the search my way. I thought I knew best, but my way left you in the hands of these thugs while you went through labor and birth. My way gave them time to steal my granddaughter.''

"Don't be so hard on yourself,'' Diana urged. "I was no different. I didn't go to the cops when I had the chance, either. I was so sure that with Ross Taylor's help I could find the men who'd stolen Alexandra and that we could get her back.''

She hugged her father again, and thought she should do it a lot more often. "We're so much alike, Dad. No wonder we have such trouble getting along. But between us both, we'll find a way to get Alexandra back.''

"You work at it,'' her mother said. "I'll just keep on praying.''

"Then we definitely can't lose.'' Diana walked between them into the living room, an arm around each of their shoulders. "I love you both,'' she said, "very, very much. I hope you always know that.''

"And we love you,'' her dad said. "We're family.''

"I know. I'm a mother myself now.''

Her dad took the easy chair. "Tell us about this Ross Taylor guy. What do we need to do to get him out of jail?''

## DAY 15

J. B. CROWE WALKED the wide corridor from his office to the conference room, his imported leather shoes sinking into the plush beige carpet. He'd called a meeting of all his top men, and before it was over, heads would roll.

Both Diana Kincaid and Ross Taylor had made him look like a fool. Thanks to the stupidity of Troy Magee and Conan. But Conan and Magee were not the only ones to blame. It was the men he'd trusted to find the right personnel so that these kinds of mistakes didn't happen. These men would have to pay the price, too, or else J.B. would lose his standing in the organization. He'd be shuffled out of the top spot, and he wasn't about to let that happen.

Even though he'd gone along with his daughter's hurry-up wedding plans, she was still insisting he give up his ties to the Texas mob. She expected him to turn his back on everything he'd worked all his adult life to achieve. But a man didn't walked away from the Mafia, not even if he wanted to. And J.B. didn't want to. Amanda would understand over time. She'd have to because he was not going to give up on her or his granddaughter. Nor would he willingly give up the power he'd worked so hard to obtain.

He stepped inside the meeting room. The silence that met him was deafening, everyone waiting to see what would happen now that the full story of Diana Kincaid's abduction and missing baby was the top story of the day. He wouldn't keep them waiting any longer.

He took his place at the head of the table, but remained standing. "It seems that some of you have decided that I'm no longer fit to run this organization. You think I've grown soft, that I let too many mistakes occur. You're wrong, and some of you will find that out very soon. For now, orders come *only* from me. I trust that's clear to all of you. If it's not, punishment will be swift and complete."

He spread his hands on the table. "Are there any questions?"

Only one man stood. A man who was already on his termination list. "What about Governor Thomas Kincaid? The man and now his daughter have made a mockery of us. And even the bomb you had planted in his office failed to detonate.''

''Neither the baby-napping debacle nor Diana's kidnapping were handled as I directed. And I was not the man who ordered the bomb. That was a stupid decision that only makes the people of Texas more eager to see Kincaid take us down. The men responsible in all these situations will pay *dearly* for their mistakes. And as for the governor and Diana Kincaid, I will *personally* handle their payback.''

The room grew silent again. His gaze took in the men at the table, one by one, before he walked to the door. ''Good day, gentlemen. Have a nice evening and sleep well, if you can.''

He pushed the door open. Amanda was standing outside. One look at her face and he knew she'd overheard his speech. He grabbed hold of her arm. ''Amanda, honey, I know how you feel.''

She jerked away from him and ran down the hall. Her earlier threat rang in his mind. She would make sure he was never a part of his granddaughter's life. She'd take his granddaughter, Susannah, and disappear from his life forever.

Pain tore at his heart. But if he had to lose his daughter and granddaughter over this, he wouldn't be the only one. Thomas Kincaid had started this war, but the final victory would belong to J. B. Crowe. No matter how empty the victory became.

*DAY 19*

THE DEFENSE ATTORNEY'S office was on the twenty-first floor of a skyscraper in downtown Dallas. His reputation was exceeded only by his bank account if the furnishings in his office were any indication. Supple leather. Rich, polished wood. Original artwork, all displayed in a corner suite that overlooked the city.

Diana and her father had been ushered in by a middle-aged secretary in a gray business suit who offered them coffee or a soft drink. They'd refused her offer, eager only to hear what the illustrious attorney had to say. He'd left a message on her father's answering machine asking if they'd come into the office to meet with him. He assured them they would be pleased with his investigation and the information he'd uncovered concerning Ross's case.

It had been eight days since Ross had turned himself in, but Diana's visits to the jail had been few and short. He seemed uncomfortable having her see him in that situation. She understood, but yet she missed him terribly.

Her father had basically put his duties as governor on hold, insisting that he was going to stay in Dallas with Diana until Alexandra was found and returned home. Their relationship had moved to a new level. Not that they didn't still argue. They were both too hardheaded to pretend to agree when they didn't, but they were making progress.

And her mom was the same sweet dear she'd always been. If anyone understood what Diana was going through as day after day passed with no word of Alexandra, she did. But Zach Logan assured them that he had a full-time team working on locating Alexandra and other babies who had been sold on the black market.

Diana had moved out of her house and into her parents' Dallas home for the time being. She needed their love and support now as much as they needed hers. Besides, she couldn't bear walking by the nursery and knowing the crib was as empty as her arms.

She looked up as Cleveland Augustus Moynihan strode through the door, smiling. "I'm glad you could both make it."

"How could we not after the phone message you left me?" Thomas said.

"I knew you'd want to hear my assessment of Ross Taylor's situation in person."

Diana leaned closer. "He's innocent, Mr. Moynihan. I'm sure he told you that."

"He has, and after my conversations with Ross and with the sheriff's department where the crime was committed, I feel I have a good handle on what really happened. Frankly, I think we have a case we can win."

"Is there a new suspect?"

"No, but I have witnesses that will attest to the fact that they saw someone hit Ross over the head and they saw him go out like a light. Another man said he saw two men he didn't recognize dragging Ross to his truck."

"Have you been able to find the men who helped him to the truck?"

"No, Governor, but I have found out that the case the Halpern sheriff put together is no more that a slipshod smattering of evidence. All they actually know is what Ross admits. He went into the bar to talk to Darrell Arnold about the paycheck that was duly owed him. They argued. Ross went back to the bar. When a fight broke out, he found himself in the thick of it so he started throwing punches to defend himself."

"So how did they come to the conclusion that he killed Darrell Arnold?"

''Much of the state's case relies on circumstantial evidence. Darrell Arnold was found about a mile down the road, slumped over in his truck with a bullet hole in his head.''

''And where was Ross during this time?''

''That's the part that bothers me most,'' Moynihan said. ''Ross woke up hours later in his truck, seventy miles away from where Mr. Arnold's body was found. His gun was missing.''

''Was it ever found?''

''The sheriff and his deputy found it the next morning, in the woods on the side of the road about a mile down from where Mr. Arnold was shot. The bullet in Mr. Arnold's head came from Ross's firearm.''

The air rushed from Diana's lungs as if someone had hit her in the chest with a club. Mr. Moynihan's idea of circumstantial evidence and hers were a long way from matching. Ross was innocent. She was sure of it, but she doubted a jury of people who didn't know him would be so convinced after they heard the evidence his lawyer was discounting as circumstantial.

Her dad was frowning, his expression hard and unyielding, the way it used to be when he'd been furious over the choices she'd made or the friends she'd chosen. She was certain he was thinking the same things now. How could he not be? The evidence all said that the man she wanted so desperately to help was a murderer.

''What makes you think you can win this case?'' her father asked. ''It sounds as if the evidence is pretty much stacked against him.''

''Stacked against him is exactly how I see it. Ross Taylor is convinced he was framed and I have to agree with him. He believes that the sheriff's intentions were to shoot him before he reached the new jail where they were supposedly taking him.''

"I've never understood that part,'' Diana admitted. "Why would the sheriff plan to kill him?''

"Unfortunately not all lawmen or judges are above the temptation of bending or breaking the law for money. That's the very reason the mob gets by with so much. They have friends in high places.''

"Is there any reason to believe the mob had a hand in this?'' Thomas asked.

"We have no proof, but that's where your money and connections will come in handy, Governor Kincaid. We'll have to conduct a thorough investigation, find out who Arnold's true enemies were.''

"But you do think that someone wanted Darrell Arnold dead?''

"It makes sense. Ross Taylor gave them the perfect opportunity to kill Arnold and put the blame on an itinerant cowboy with no alibi. That's one of the reasons I believe Ross Taylor's story. Everything is too pat, too easy. A man who can't remember driving to a spot seventy miles away from where he passed out makes me think that someone gave him something to make sure he stayed knocked out. A gun found the very next morning, not a mile from the scene of the crime reeks of the fact that it was probably planted. A perfect setup.''

"Or an imperfect murder,'' her dad said, his hands clasped around the leather briefcase he held in his lap.

"What about bail?'' Diana asked. "Has it been set?''

"Men accused of murder seldom get the opportunity to post bail, but due to the circumstances, the judge has made an exception in this case.''

"What circumstances are those?'' Thomas asked before Diana had the chance.

"He was a hero in the bust of the baby-selling ring. He led your daughter to safety when he could have run. And even though he escaped from a sheriff he didn't trust, he willingly contacted Zach Logan and turned himself in. None of those are the actions of a cold-blooded killer."

"What is the amount of bail?" Diana asked again. She wanted Ross out of jail, wanted him home with her.

"One million dollars."

She jumped from her chair, anger tearing away her control. She didn't have a million dollars cash and she knew Ross had no way of raising that kind of money. "One million dollars. Is that all? Why not ask for the moon and a couple of stars? Or maybe we could throw in the Alamo. Ask the judge that for me, will you?"

"Let it go, Diana." Her dad stood and put a hand on her shoulder, hoping to quiet her, she was sure, but she would not be quieted.

"Some slimeball held me prisoner for two weeks and then stole my daughter so that he could sell her on the black market the way he was selling other women's babies. I read that he was released on bail yesterday. What do you want to bet that he did not have to put up a million dollars bond?"

"I'll have the check to you by this afternoon."

She turned and stared at her dad, sure she had to have heard him wrong. But he was extending his hand to the attorney and smiling.

"It's a lot of money, but my daughter says Ross Taylor's innocent and that he can be trusted. I respect her judgment. Besides, he saved her life."

You could have bowled her over with a feather. But she was damn proud that Governor Thomas Kincaid was her dad.

ROSS'S FIRST STOP after being released from jail was the Dallas home of Governor and Mrs. Kincaid. His jail cell had been cramped, dark and depressing. The Kincaid home was opulent, palatial and imposing. He had never felt more out of place in his life.

"Just dinner," Diana assured him, as she gave him a quick tour of the house, "then we can cut out and go to my place."

She walked in front of him, looking absolutely stunning in a blue dress that dipped just low enough in front to get his juices running and then swung seductively around her shapely legs. The double string of pearls around her neck looked like the real thing, not that he was an expert on jewelry. "I don't think I'm dressed for dinner," he said. "I don't think I've ever been as dressed for dinner as you are."

She stopped and let her gaze walk from the open collar of his cotton shirt to the hem of his worn jeans. "You look terrific."

"You're definitely prejudiced."

"You better believe it." She stepped beside him and cuffed her hand around his behind. "I'll show you just how much later tonight."

"I'll hold you to that." And he'd love every minute of it, but it wouldn't change the facts. He couldn't move into this lifestyle. He wouldn't fit.

He'd loved his life as a cop, being in the thick of things, having a beer with the guys in a neighborhood bar. And after he'd been fired from the force, he'd gone back to the life of a cowboy, the only other life he knew, and that wasn't bad either. But, luxury? It wasn't him.

Not that he didn't want Diana. He was crazy about her. He'd never known a woman who could be so totally feminine and still tough as a wild bull when she had to be. He loved the way she laughed and even the way she cried. The way she fought and fought and kept on fighting to find her baby and to keep him from spending the rest of his life in jail.

Plain and simple, he loved Diana. But it wasn't going to work.

"And this is the dining room," she said, propping a hip against the door frame. "I'm not sure what we're having for dinner tonight, but I'm certain Jacques has planned something extra special just for you. He can't wait to meet you."

"And Jacques would be…?"

"The cook. He's been with the family for years. He travels back and forth between here and the governor's mansion in Austin. Dad is convinced that everyone else's cooking gives him heartburn."

Ross wondered if Jacques knew how to grill a sirloin to perfection the way he did, but he didn't ask. He also wondered if Diana had ever eaten food cooked over an open fire with only the stars over her head, and he realized how much he wished they were doing that tonight. Just the two of them. Without the array of silver, crystal and china spread out on the table in front of them now.

"Looks like we might be going to drink our way through dinner. Four glasses per person and none of them a beer mug."

She stopped and looked up at him. The house and the clothes were different. The look was the Diana he knew. His heart did a less than manly somersault.

"I know this isn't your style, Ross, but having you here tonight is important to my parents. They're in-

debted to you for all you've done for me and for trying
to help me find Alexandra.''

The way she said her daughter's name touched his
heart. No matter how upbeat she seemed, part of her
was missing and would be until she was reunited with
Alexandra.

He put an arm around her waist. "I'll do you proud.
I may use the wrong fork from time to time, but I won't
make fun or complain. I really do appreciate what you
and your dad are doing for me. Without you, I'd be
eating jail cuisine tonight and sleeping on a lumpy cot.''

She reached up and touched her lips to his. "I promise you no lumps. I don't promise you a lot of sleep.''

"Who needs it?''

By the time they'd made their rounds of the house,
her parents were waiting for them in the parlor. This
was not his cup of tea, or flute of champagne as the
case may be, but he'd play the game as long as he could
or until Diana came to her senses and kicked him out.
The day would come, as soon as she realized that the
cowboy who'd found her in the woods couldn't be
housebroken, at least not enough for a house like this.

THE DINNER went better than Ross had expected. He'd
met the governor a few days earlier, in the attorney's
office, but the mood on that occasion had not been con-
ducive to getting to know a man. He'd liked him a lot
better tonight. And he loved Diana's mother. She was
a good woman by any man's standards. But like Diana,
neither of her parents would rest easy until Alexandra
was found and back home.

Now Ross and Diana were back at her place. He lay
in the king-size bed, the sheets luxurious, his head
propped up on down-filled pillows. The overhead lights

were off, the room lit by a cluster of candles that emitted a fragrance he couldn't identify.

Before tonight, they'd made love in a dingy motel room. It had been Diana who had brought all the magic to those occasions, lit up the room, made the experience one he'd never forget. He'd thought about those nights constantly during his week in jail. It had been the only good thing he had to hold on to.

He hadn't been nervous in the motel room, but here in the huge bed, with candles burning and soft music playing, he felt a little intimidated, like a bridegroom expected to make the wedding night memorable for his new bride. Only he didn't have any tricks up his sleeve, any moves different than the ones he'd already used.

Diana opened the door and stepped into the bedroom, a silky white negligee setting off her ivory skin and red hair. And Ross forgot the size of her house and the opulence of the furnishings. Forgot that she wore pearls and he wore denims. Forgot everything except Diana and knew he'd always remember the way she looked right now.

# Chapter Seventeen

Ross pulled Diana down beside him and found her mouth with his. And once his lips and hands were on her, he couldn't let go.

They rolled together, their legs entangled, their bodies sliding against each other, the sultry friction like erogenous strokes of fire on his flesh.

"I thought I had only dreamed it was this good with you," he whispered, "but this is a million times better than my dreams."

"I've missed you so much, Ross. Every day, every night. I've ached to crawl into your arms."

"It was that way for me, too." He kissed her lips, her neck, then buried his face in her luscious breasts. She smelled of honeysuckle, tasted only of Diana. He suckled each nipple, cupped the soft mounds of her breasts in his hands, taking his time before he moved lower, tasting and nibbling his way across the soft curves of her stomach.

He loved that she wasn't ashamed of her body, didn't blow out the candles so that they made love in the dark. He liked seeing her, knowing he was the one she wanted here in her bed.

His hands caressed the rounded fullness of her hips,

then explored her entire body. "I don't want to hurt you."

"It's still too soon for penetration. The doctor said to wait six weeks, but I seem to have healed fine."

"You seem perfect to me."

"And you feel perfect." She kissed his shoulders and tangled her fingers in his hair pulling him close. "I never thought I'd feel this way again. So loved. So right."

And loving Diana was right. It was the living in her world that would be all wrong. But he refused to think of that now, refused to think at all. He stroked her smooth flesh and brushed his lips across her breasts and abdomen. She called his name, then took his hand and guided it down her stomach to the triangle of heated passion.

He touched her gently, the heat rising inside him in waves as tiny moans of pleasure gurgled from her throat. She jerked, muscles taut, then arched toward him, wrapping her legs around him and holding him close as her body shook in release.

He hadn't expected her to climax so quickly, but he could understand it. Already the blood was running so hot inside him, he could barely hold back the explosion that was sure to come.

She touched his erection, caressed it, held it against her stomach. "I can't wait until the day I can feel you inside me," she whispered. "I want us to be one, complete."

"I am complete, Diana. For the first time in my life, I'm totally complete."

"I love you." Her words were a murmur, a caress. She touched and stroked and carried him over the top. When he started the plunge back to earth, he held her close and wished he never had to let her go, wished he could hold back the dawn and all the new problems it would bring.

But he was a realist. So he'd just enjoy heaven while it lay in his arms, knowing it couldn't last forever.

## DAY 20

ROSS SAT at the outdoor table on Diana's patio devouring the Western omelet she'd set in front of him. A bluebird fluttered to the feeder a few feet away and a squirrel scurried across the lawn and up the trunk of a large oak tree. "You have a great place here."

"I've always liked it, but now I'm thinking of selling the house."

"You'd leave a lot of memories behind."

"I'd pack the good ones and take them with me. The bad ones I'd be all too happy to desert." She reached across the table and linked her fingers with his. "My husband and I were happy, Ross. I loved him and he loved me. But he's been dead almost two years. I want to go on with my life."

"You should."

"When I said I loved you last night, I meant it. It's different from the way I loved Alex. Wilder, more passionate, more unpredictable. Maybe it's because we're so different, or maybe it's the way we met. I don't know and I don't care. I only know that I can't imagine life without you."

The tension swelled inside him, tight and choking. A woman saying I love you shouldn't do that to him. Maybe it wouldn't if he had anything to offer her, but he didn't.

"I know you think you love me, Diana, and maybe

you do, but love can't wipe away differences as great as the ones that separate us." He was crazy, turning down the one thing he wanted more than he'd ever wanted anything in his life, but it was the way it had to be. Better to walk out in the beginning than try to build a life with her only to have it come tumbling down around him. "I can give you *now*. I can't promise forever."

"You're a hard man, Ross Taylor."

"I'm a man who still has a murder trial hanging over my head. And even if I'm cleared, that kind of thing follows you around for a long, long time."

The phone rang. He was glad. A minute more of holding hands and staring into her eyes and he might lose what little good sense he had left. He could see himself bending on one knee on the brick patio, proposing marriage. Of course, he'd have to buy a cigar or a box of Cracker Jack to get a ring.

"It's for you," she said. "It's Dylan Garrett."

He left his eggs for the birds and took the call.

DIANA STOOD at the closed door to the nursery. It was the first time she'd been here alone since before the abduction. Ross had offered to take her to her parents while he went to lunch with Dylan, but she couldn't avoid being in the house alone forever, couldn't avoid the nursery she'd planned for Alexandra.

There was no reason to go inside, but she couldn't help herself. She turned the knob and pushed the door, still hesitant. Finally she stepped into the room. Strange that it would be just as she'd left it when nothing else about her life was the same.

The lace-trimmed bassinet sat beneath the wide window, catching the sunbeams that filtered through the pink gingham curtains. A musical mobile of swaying Dalmatians hung over the crib and the teddy bear sat in the corner, watching over it all. Waiting for Alexandra to come home.

The phone rang. She ignored it. She was in no mood to talk to anyone right now, not even her mother. The answering machine would pick up, and if it was an emergency, she'd answer then.

Backing toward the door, she listened for a voice to come from the answering machine. But it wasn't a voice. It was the muted sound of crying. A baby.

She ran down the hall and yanked the receiver from the cradle. "If this is some sick joke, you should be ashamed of yourself. Do you know what it's like to—"

"This is no joke."

The crying had stopped. It was a woman's voice on the line now, low, a little shaky.

"Who is this and what do you want?"

"Is this Diana Kincaid?"

"Yes. I'm Diana. Who are you?"

"I'm the woman who bought your baby. I didn't know. They told me the mother didn't want her, couldn't take care of her."

Diana went weak. She held on to the table for support. She'd waited for this call, but now that it had come, she was afraid to believe it was real. "How do you know about me?"

"From the stories in the newspaper. You're the woman who busted the baby ring. Those weren't the men who delivered my baby, but I paid for her all the same. Seventy thousand dollars. We mortgaged our house, but she's worth it. She's so precious. I already love her."

"What makes you think this is my child?"

"It said in the paper that your baby's name was Alexandra. When the two men brought her to me, they said the baby's mother had named her Alexandra, but that I could give her a new name if I wanted. I call her Suzette. I always liked that name."

"Please, tell me who you are. Tell me where you live. If you have my baby, you have to give her back. She's my flesh and blood. I carried her inside me."

"I know. But the men told me I should never tell anyone how I got her. They made me promise. And now that I've read what they did to you, I'm afraid to cross them."

"No, don't be afraid. The police will protect you. You have to tell me how to find you."

"The police didn't protect you. But I'll give you your baby if you'll do this my way. I can't keep her, knowing she was stolen from you."

"I'll do whatever you say. I can come and get her. You won't even have to leave your house."

"You can't come here. Those men might find out. We'll have to meet somewhere else, and you'll have to promise to come alone. If you don't, you won't see me or the baby when you get here."

"I'll come alone. I'll do anything you say. Just tell me when and where."

"To your father's ranch."

"I don't understand."

"I live near there and it's a place we both can find."

"Shall I meet you at the front gate?"

"No. Come down the back road, the one that crosses Cutcheons River."

"I know that area well. I used to ride out that way."

"Then you know right where the old red barn is."

"I do. Dad still keeps extra hay in there."

"Be there in one hour, Diana. But come alone. I want to give you back your baby, but you have to protect me. I don't want to be kidnapped and carried off the way you were."

"I'll be there, but please don't leave if I'm late. Sometimes the traffic is bad going out of town."

The woman didn't say a word, but Diana could hear the baby crying in the background. It was Alexandra. She was sure of it. She hung up the phone. She needed to call Ross and let him know where she was going, but she had no clue where he and Dylan had gone for lunch.

He wouldn't want her to go alone. He'd think it was dangerous. She knew it was, but it was a chance she had to take. He'd be home soon. She'd leave him a message where to find her, but she couldn't wait on him. This woman was scared to death, and it wouldn't take much to send her running.

She scribbled a note on a sheet of paper and left it by the phone. Anticipation rushed her senses, urged her to hurry, but she put down enough details that Ross would know where she'd gone and how to find her.

*Let this be for real,* she prayed, as she grabbed her purse and keys and ran out the door. But in her heart she knew it was. When she got to the barn Alexandra would be there. She was absolutely sure of it.

THE TRAFFIC in town was horrendous. Diana dodged in and out of lines of slow-moving cars, rushing ahead in spurts only to stop and wait when the snarl became unmovable. She called her house a couple of times, hoping to catch Ross, but evidently the lunch had lasted longer than he'd anticipated, or maybe he'd already gotten her message and started toward the ranch himself.

Finally she came to the bridge that crossed Cutcheons

River. Half the year it was more of a creek than a river, but it was running high now, the result of spring rains. One more mile. She could see the barn. Her heart pounded. The blood rushed to her head. There was no staying calm now. If this was for real, Alexandra could be in her arms in minutes.

She pulled onto the dirt road that led to the barn. Stopping the car, she jumped out and opened the gate. She hated to take the time to close it again, but there were cows in the pasture, and if she left it open they'd wander onto the road.

Her hands shook on the wheel, but somehow she made it to the barn. She killed the engine, jumped from the car and ran through the open doors.

And then her heart leaped clear to her throat. Alexandra was there, wrapped in a blanket, lying inside a plastic clothes basket. She raced across the hay-strewn earth, stooped to pick her up. But it wasn't a baby at all. It was a cold, lifeless doll. A heartlessly cruel trick, and she'd fallen for it.

She turned round and round in the middle of the barn, looking for someone to blame, someone to lash out at. "Why are you doing this to me?" The cry reverberated off the walls and ceiling and flew back into her face.

The barn door banged shut behind her. Apprehension shot through her system.

"Diana Kincaid. You're quite a woman. A chip off the old block."

She turned, her stomach churning, fear wrapping cold fingers around her heart. "Mr. Crowe. What are you doing here?"

# Chapter Eighteen

J. B. Crowe stared at Diana from across the barn. "How nice of you to meet me here."

The man standing in front of her was definitely J. B. Crowe, but he was not the polished gentleman she'd met at charity functions. This man was cold, hard. Evil. It was in his eyes and in his voice.

"It was you who had me kidnapped, wasn't it? You're the one who stole my baby."

"I had you kidnapped. The mistake was in not having you killed."

"I want my baby back."

"Oh, I'm sure you do. Then you and Ross Taylor can be one happy family. Thomas would like that, too. He'd have his daughter and granddaughter close by. You could have Sunday dinners together, just like a real family."

"You have a daughter, Mr. Crowe, and a granddaughter."

"I *did* have a daughter and granddaughter. Until Thomas Kincaid ran them away with his accusations and threats."

"You chose the life of a criminal. No one made you."

"Did you hear that from your father? He was always full of wonderful advice and never was one to let well enough alone." He reached under his jacket and pulled out a pistol.

"Please. I know you're upset with my dad, but killing me won't solve anything."

"It will satisfy me, Diana. That's why I had you come here. I want your dad to find you dead on his own land."

"You are a very sick man, Mr. Crowe."

He aimed the pistol at her head. Her stomach pitched and rocked sickeningly. She had to do something, had to stop him. She searched the area frantically, but the only weapon in sight was a pitchfork, and it was too far away for her to reach.

But Alexandra was still out there somewhere and she needed her mother. Diana stared at the lifeless doll, then let her gaze move to Crowe's taunting smirk as he pointed the gun at her head. Staring him straight in the eye, she hooked her toe around the basket and kicked it toward him.

It left the ground like a missile, hurling toward his head. He ducked but fired anyway. The bullet burrowed into the wooden beam over her head with a splintering crack. But he still held the gun, and she was out of surprises.

"I guess this is it, Diana. The Kincaids lose. *I* win."

"Kill me, if it makes you happy, but please don't kill my baby." She fell to her knees, pleading. "Wherever she is, have them take care of her."

"That's out of my hands."

The barn door flew open. J. B. Crowe spun around and fired before he had time to process who was standing in the door. The bullet hit with a force that sent

Amanda Crowe stumbling and then falling to the ground.

"Amanda! No! Nooo!" Crowe dropped the gun and rushed toward his daughter, falling on top of her, calling her name over and over.

"I begged you to stop, but you wouldn't listen. You have to let this go. You have to give yourself up."

"I didn't mean to hurt you. Not you, Amanda. I never meant to hurt you."

Tears poured from Diana's eyes as she watched the scene in front of her. She stooped to pick up the gun. Before she could, Dylan, Ross and Zach Logan walked through the door.

"What happened here?" Zach asked.

No one answered. But Ross rushed toward her, took her in his arms and held her as if he'd never let her go. And that was perfectly fine with Diana.

Ross STOOD BESIDE Diana as the ambulance carrying Amanda Crowe pulled through the back gate of the ranch. Zach Logan and Dylan Garrett followed it in a police cruiser, carrying J. B. Crowe to jail.

Diana waited until the ambulance had disappeared from sight before turning back toward the barn. "Poor thing. She'd followed her father here, only wanting to beg him one more time to give this up before it was too late."

"And still she probably saved your life."

"It was a big cost to pay. For her and for Crowe. She'll recover, but I wonder if he'll ever get over putting a bullet through his own daughter."

"He'll have plenty of time. I don't think there's any way he'll get off without a jail sentence this time."

"And in spite of everything, Amanda loves him. I heard her tell him so."

Ross took her hand and led her into the sunshine. "I'm just glad I got here when I did. Otherwise, he might still have decided to kill you."

"You must have driven like crazy once you got the message I left you."

His eyebrows arched. "I never got a message."

"Then how did you know where to find me?"

"Zach Logan had someone watching your house. He saw you leave and tried to keep up with you, but he lost you in the traffic. He'd called us and alerted us that you'd disappeared."

"If he lost me, I still don't see how you ended up at the ranch."

"We rushed to the scene where he'd last seen you. That's when Dylan spied Amanda Crowe speeding down the highway toward your ranch. We tried to follow her on a hunch that J.B. might be up to something. We lost her in the traffic as well, but Zach knew your family had a ranch out here. We drove until we spotted your car and Amanda's. We never saw Crowe's. He'd hidden it too well."

"And now he's finally in custody. The war is over, but I still don't have my baby." She leaned into him. "Take me home, Ross. I want to get out of here. I don't think I'll ever be able to walk into this barn again without reliving this day."

"I'll take you home, but we need to make a stop first."

"Can't it wait?"

"I don't think so. You see, Dylan got a call while we were having lunch."

She groaned. "Not more bad news. Not today."

"It could be good. Dylan and Lily had a woman working for them, a temporary employee named Jane Bateman. She got a lead on a baby-napping ring and went to check it out. She grabbed the baby and escaped with it, but she was hurt in the ruckus. Anyway, to make a long story short, she escaped from the men and finally recovered enough to get in touch with Dylan. She still has this baby."

"There's no reason to think it's Alexandra."

"The timing is right. I think you should check it out."

She turned away. "But what if it isn't? I don't know if I can stand to get my hopes up again only to have them shattered along with my heart."

"I'll be with you, if that's worth anything."

"It means a lot, but I'm not even sure that's enough to get me through another heartbreaking disappointment. Did Jane Bateman describe the baby?"

"Female. Healthy. Red hair. About seven and a half pounds."

She took a deep breath, garnering all her strength. "When can we see her?"

"Jane's on a plane right now, flying the baby to Dallas. She should be at the hotel by the time we get there."

"Then I guess we better get started."

He wrapped an arm around her shoulders and led her to the car, hoping against hope that this was Alexandra. If any woman ever deserved a break, it was Diana Kincaid.

DIANA STOOD BESIDE Ross while he knocked at the door to the hotel room where Jane Bateman and somebody's baby were waiting. This morning she would have rushed through the door, confident that the baby would be Alexandra.

But that last defeat had taken its toll. J. B. Crowe had taken a toll. She'd always known evil existed, but up until the past few weeks, she'd never come face-to-face with people like that.

But as bad as J. B. Crowe had been in his life, he'd also had some good in him. If he hadn't, he couldn't have loved his daughter so much. And he did love her. His anguish when she'd taken the bullet from his gun had been all too real.

The door to the hotel room opened.

"I'm Ross Taylor and this is Diana Kincaid."

"I'm Jane Bateman," the woman whispered, then put a finger to her lips. "The baby's in the carriage, but she's just fallen asleep, and it's not a good idea to wake her. She already has a temper. It's the red hair, I guess."

Diana tiptoed across the room, her insides fluttering like crazy. All she had to do was peek inside the baby carriage and she would know. Some people claimed that all babies looked alike, but Diana didn't believe that. She had memorized every delicate feature in that brief time she'd held her daughter.

She took Ross's hand and he squeezed it.

"Time to look," he said.

She leaned over the carriage and then blinked fast, making sure she wasn't dreaming. "It's her. It's Alexandra." Sleeping or not, temper or not, she didn't care. She picked her up and cuddled her against her chest, against her heart. Tears streamed down her cheeks. "Mommy has you back, sweetheart. And Mommy and Ross will take you home."

Ross flicked a hand across his eyes. They were smarting bad and watering like crazy. He figured he must be catching a cold.

"ROSS TAYLOR CAUGHT a glimpse of himself in the mirror over the mantel. He had to look twice to make sure it was really him. A black bow tie and stiff collar. Even a cummerbund around his waist. Ross Taylor partying at the governor's mansion in tails. Who'd have ever thought it?

"Admiring yourself?" Diana asked, slipping up behind him.

"Not now that I have you to admire."

"Careful now, flattery will get you anywhere."

"Including out of these duds."

"As soon as the party's over."

And that couldn't be too soon for him. Someone in the next room tapped on the rim of a champagne glass.

"I think it's time for speeches and accolades," Diana said, slipping her hand in his. "We need to go into the main room."

He trailed along beside her. By the time they reached party central, Governor Kincaid was behind the podium, looking out over the crowd. He was holding Alexandra in his arms and looking very proud and grandfatherly. And why not? The DNA testing had been completed. The baby in his arms was definitely a Kincaid. Not that Diana had ever had a doubt.

"As you know, the party tonight is to celebrate the return of my granddaughter," the governor said, holding her up so everyone could have a look. "We all went through some difficult times in the past few weeks, especially Diana, but all that's behind us now, thanks to a lot of good men and a couple of very brave women. But before I get started, we have another man who'd like to say a few words tonight. Zach Logan, the mike is all yours.''

Zach Logan replaced the governor at the podium. He was grinning from ear to ear, but he looked a lot more comfortable in his tux than Ross felt. Maybe dealing with this high-society stuff got easier with age.

''I just want to say that I've headed up the antimob task force for five years now. It was always one step forward and two steps backward. All of that changed this week. A big thanks for that goes to Ross Taylor and Diana Kincaid. If they hadn't busted the baby-napping ring and gotten all of this started, I wouldn't be standing up here tonight telling you that J. B. Crowe has admitted his role as the leader of organized crime in the state of Texas and the southwestern part of the United States.''

The crowd broke into applause. Ross joined them. It was a big step. He'd longed to see Crowe get what he had coming to him for years, lived on the anger and the need for revenge. But recently, he'd learned that love was a much better bedfellow than hate.

And as evil as Crowe was, he was still only one man in an organization of men ruled by greed. His arrest might bend the Mafia a little, but it wouldn't break them. They'd already be jockeying for who would climb up the ladder and take Crowe's place. And he wouldn't be a bit surprised if Crowe didn't try to hold on to some of his power from his jail cell. It had been done before in cases like this.

''Ross Taylor, where are you?''

Somewhere else, Ross wished, as he heard his ex-boss call his name. But he turned and waved to Zach.

''Step over here with me for a minute. Diana, you

come with him. I have some news that the two of you don't even know about.''

Diana took Ross's hand and dragged him to the podium. He hated attention in a crowd like this. If there was anything good at all about the moment, it was the fact that he was holding the hand of the prettiest woman in the room.

''Ross Taylor used to work for me,'' Zach said. ''His one goal back then was to nail J. B. Crowe. But in the process, he made a powerful enemy of the man. So powerful that when Ross showed up back in Texas, Crowe decided to get rid of him and make sure he wasn't blamed for the murder. So he framed Ross for the murder of a man who'd crossed him, a Texas rancher named Darrell Arnold. The next move was to have Ross shot in an orchestrated escape attempt. He thought it would get Ross Taylor out of his hair for good, but it didn't work that way. As of tonight, thanks to Troy Magee's testimony in a plea-bargaining situation, all charges have been dropped against Ross Taylor.''

Ross was stunned into silence. Diana cheered and threw her arms around his neck. He heard only bits and pieces of the rest of the speech. ''A special thanks to Amanda Crowe for having the foresight to pick up the phone and overhear a conversation between her dad and his right-hand man. That's how she knew where he was heading when he lured Diana to the barn. She was a very brave lady and everyone is grateful that a full recovery is expected. Her new husband Jesse Brock will be beside her every step of the way. And then there are kudos to Dylan Garrett for his role in helping to nab the Mafia kingpin.''

When Zach stepped away from the podium, Diana

rose up on tiptoe and kissed Ross, right in front of God and everybody. "Maybe the evil and the enmity between my dad and Crowe has finally been put to rest," she said. "And no more excuses that you're a man with a jail sentence over your head. Not that I needed anyone's testimony to convince me you were innocent."

Alexandra started to fuss and Governor Kincaid handed his granddaughter to Diana and went back to finish his speech. He left nobody out in his words of praise, not even Jane Bateman, though she'd declined his invitation to attend the party. She'd already resigned her position with Finders Keepers and gone back to the ranch of the man who had helped her when she'd been injured saving Diana's baby.

Once the speech was over, Diana roamed the room showing off her daughter amidst the tinkle of glasses and music and laughter. Anne had insisted her husband throw the party in the very early evening so that it wouldn't interfere with Alexandra's bedtime. Ross was sure that a more doting grandmother had never lived.

The Kincaids. More than he'd expected them to be. Way more, but they were still too rich for his blood. He might be sporting black tie and tails, but when the finery came off, he'd still be just Ross Taylor. Cowboy or maybe even cop if Zach would offer him his job back now that his record was clean.

But he was going to miss Diana Kincaid for the rest of his life.

He walked past the partiers, down the hall and to the guest bedroom where he'd exchanged his jeans for the rented tuxedo. There was nothing wrong with formal dress and cocktail parties. They just weren't for him.

He started to work on the necktie. The door opened

behind him and Diana stepped inside, closing the door behind her. "Going somewhere, pard'ner?"

God, how he hated goodbyes. "It seemed like the time to jump on my horse and ride into the sunset."

"I thought you might have something like that in mind." She pulled her right hand from behind her back, dangling a pair of handcuffs.

He backed away. "No funny stuff, Diana."

"I'm not laughing." Her eyes sparkled like emeralds in sunshine. "I'll be a cop's wife, a cowboy's wife, or any kind of wife you need me to be, Ross Taylor, but I am not losing my man. So which is it? A wedding ring or these?" She shook the metal cuffs in front of him like bells.

"Do you ever give up?"

"Not when the cause is important. You should know that about me by now." She stepped closer, the handcuffs still in hand. "And as you know, I come as a package deal. Me and Alexandra, two for the price of one." She reached behind her back and started unzipping her dress, letting it slide from her slender shoulders.

He groaned. "Talk about not playing fair."

The dress slid down her body and pooled at her feet. "A wedding ring, or these," she taunted, still dangling the cuffs. "Your call."

He spread his hands, palms up. "I haven't lied to you, Diana. What you see is what you get."

She stepped closer. "I hope so. Boy, do I hope so." Kicking out of her shoes, she wrapped her arms around him. "I love you so much that I can't imagine life without you. And I plan to keep on loving you forever. You, Ross Taylor. Just the way you are."

He shook his head. No one could win against Diana

Kincaid once she set her mind to something. And a man would have to be a fool to want to. He took the handcuffs from her hands and tossed them to the bed, then walked over and locked the bedroom door.

Ross Taylor was a lot of things, but he was nobody's fool.

*Isabella Trueblood made history reuniting people torn apart by war and an epidemic. Now, generations later, Lily and Dylan Garrett carry on her work with their agency, Finders Keepers. Circumstances may have changed, but the goal remains the same.*

*The legend continues with the first book in our exciting new continuity series,*

## TRUEBLOOD, TEXAS

*A year's worth of stories where long lost relatives are reunited and new lovers find each other.*

*Watch for*

### THE COWBOY WANTS A BABY

*by Jo Leigh*

*Coming next month*

*Here's a preview!*

*Ailing Eve Bishop desperately wants to find her estranged grandson and heir before she dies. Lily Garrett is on the case. Now all Lily has to do is find a way to hog-tie a lone wolf and get him back to Grandma's house. Gossip says that dangerously handsome Cole Bishop is going to pay someone to have his child, which gives this Little Red Riding Hood an idea....*

# CHAPTER ONE

LILY CLOSED her bedroom door, then slumped against it, her heart beating frenziedly against her chest. "I am in *so* much trouble here. And I've only known him three hours."

She pushed off the door and flung herself across the bed. That little tango in the kitchen had nearly done her in. The jerk had some nerve testing her like that. For all he knew, she was going to be the mother of his child. It wasn't nice and it wasn't fair, and oh, my God, how she'd flunked.

This attraction to him was something outside of her experience. Her body had never reacted like it just had with Cole.

She turned over and looked down at her boobs. "Bad body," she scolded. But there were no immediate apologies. Maybe she should call Dylan and talk it over with him. No. This was not something she wished to discuss with her brother. Ashley? Uh-uh. Somehow, somewhere, it would come back and bite her on the butt.

The other options were her two closest girlfriends, Denise and Sandy, but Denise was in Europe on a business trip and Sandy was too much in love with Paul, her babe du jour, to give sensible advice.

What a pickle. The intelligent thing would be to march out there, tell Cole that she was a private detective, that she'd been sent by Eve, yada, yada, yada. Then he'd tell her exactly what she could do with Finders Keepers, and she'd be staying at the Jessup Motel.

Plan B? Keep her wits about her, find out all she could about Cole, and when the time was right, explain the situation if it seemed prudent. If he really was a nutball, she didn't want to turn him on Eve.

And then there was Plan C. Which was forget about the case, forget about her vow to stay chaste until she was completely over Jason, and attack Cole in the middle of the night. Make love until the paramedics were called, then spring her true mission on him when he was too weak to argue.

Plan C had some merit. She just wished she'd paid attention when Sandy had talked about rebound guys. There was something every woman should know about meeting men right after a big breakup, but for the life of her, Lily couldn't remember what it was. Sleep with them? Don't sleep with them? It was one of the two.

My goodness, but this was not how she thought her day was going to go. However, there was a little part of her that was unapologetically excited. Curious as hell about what was going to happen next. She honestly didn't know. Would he make another move? Would he ignore her?

She had the feeling if he really meant to kick her out she would have been kicked out by now. No, despite the Granite Man demeanor, the guy was probably as confused as she was.

Wanting to hire a wife. For heaven's sake. What a dumb thing to do. Maybe she was supposed to be here to knock some sense into the big guy. Show him that he couldn't be in control of everything. And that money and the love of a mother didn't mix.

Sighing, she sat up, looked at the clock. Another forty minutes and it would be dinner. She was definitely hungry. But there was time to shower, to cool herself down and gather her composure. Assuming, that is, that she could stop thinking about those shoulders.

# *Psst...*

**HARLEQUIN®**
**INTRIGUE®**

has an even *bigger* secret—

but it's ***confidential***

till September 2001!

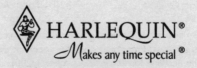

*Harlequin truly does make any time special. . . . This year we are celebrating weddings in style!*

To help us celebrate, we want you to tell us how wearing the Harlequin wedding gown will make your wedding day special. As the grand prize, Harlequin will offer one lucky bride the chance to **"Walk Down the Aisle"** in the Harlequin wedding gown!

### There's more...

For her honeymoon, she and her groom will spend five nights at the **Hyatt Regency Maui.** As part of this five-night honeymoon at the hotel renowned for its romantic attractions, the couple will enjoy a candlelit dinner for two in Swan Court, a sunset sail on the hotel's catamaran, and duet spa treatments.

Maui • Molokai • Lanai

To enter, please write, in, 250 words or less, how wearing the Harlequin wedding gown will make your wedding day special. The entry will be judged based on its emotionally compelling nature, its originality and creativity, and its sincerity. This contest is open to Canadian and U.S. residents only and to those who are 18 years of age and older. There is no purchase necessary to enter. Void where prohibited. See further contest rules attached. Please send your entry to:

### Walk Down the Aisle Contest

| In Canada | In U.S.A. |
|---|---|
| P.O. Box 637 | P.O. Box 9076 |
| Fort Erie, Ontario | 3010 Walden Ave. |
| L2A 5X3 | Buffalo, NY 14269-9076 |

You can also enter by visiting www.eHarlequin.com
***Win the Harlequin wedding gown and the vacation of a lifetime!***
The deadline for entries is October 1, 2001.

*Makes any time special* ®

PHWDACONT1

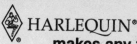

In August 2001
New York Times bestselling author

# TESS GERRITSEN

joins

## ANNETTE BROADRICK

&

## Mary Lynn Baxter

in

# TAKE5

Volume 4

These five riveting love stories are
quick reads, great escapes and
guarantee five times the suspense.

## Plus

With $5.00 worth of coupons inside,
this is one *exciting* deal!

HARLEQUIN®
*Makes any time special* ®

Visit us at www.eHarlequin.com                    HNCPV4R